Arabian Vengeance

A Pat Walsh Thriller

James Lawrence

Arabian Vengeance is a work of fiction. Apart from the events and locales that figure in the narrative, all names, characters, places, and incidents are the products of the author's imagination or are used fictitiously. Any resemblance to current events, locales, or living persons is entirely coincidental.

ISBN-13: 978-1976063213
ISBN-10: 1976063213

Dedication

This book is dedicated to my wife and family.
Without their support and assistance,
it would not have been possible to complete this book.

About the Author

James Lawrence has been a soldier, small business owner, military advisor, and international arms dealer. He is the author of *Lost in Arabia* and he currently lives and works in the Middle East.

Men should be either treated generously or destroyed, because they take revenge for slight injuries—for heavy ones they cannot.

—Niccolo Machiavelli

Chapter 1

Brussels, Belgium

Ahmed Eleiwi zipped his leather jacket against the wind as he exited the Bruxelles Central Train Station and entered downtown Brussels. It was a Saturday afternoon and the station was crowded with visitors on their way to enjoy a sunny spring afternoon shopping and sightseeing in the Grand Place Square. As he passed through the main doors of the station, he drew a second look from one of the soldiers positioned in the entryway. Belgium's response to the reoccurring terrorist incidents over the past year had been to station hundreds of military personnel throughout the city. In the congested downtown Brussels area, it was becoming increasingly difficult for a man Middle Eastern in appearance to travel unmolested. Ahmed was purposely carrying no bags to avoid arousing too much suspicion. Despite his efforts, the soldier signaled for him to come over and gave him a quick pat-down from top to bottom. Ahmed reminded himself that it was just a random search and forced himself to remain calm.

Despite his heart kicking into high gear, Ahmed slowly walked away from the guard and continued at a leisurely pace past the Hilton Grand Place Hotel and through the arch passageway, taking him into the square proper. As he entered the Grand Place, Ahmed stopped to get his bearings. Along one side of the rectangular cobblestone square, a rock band was playing on a stage set up against a building wall, midway along one of the sides. It was early afternoon, and the UNESCO World Heritage site was crowded with a festival atmosphere. Tourist guides hustled to corral their charges across the expanse to the many historical and architectural items of interest. It was Earth Day, and several hundred protestors, still wearing green shirts and carrying signs from the morning march, congregated near the stage. The protestors were drinking beer, dancing to the music and having a great time in the unseasonably cool weather.

The small square was bordered by four- and five-story gothic buildings made of grey stone and adorned with gold accents, archways and magnificent spires. He searched for the City Hall, with its distinctive nighty-six-meter tower holding the Archangel Michael. Having found his bearings, he confirmed he was in the northeast corner.

Ahmed looked west and found the Hard Rock Café sign only fifty meters from his location. He checked his cell phone and found a text: "3rd Floor, window." Ahmed stepped inside the narrow restaurant entryway and walked through the souvenir shop to the hostess. Before she could offer to help him, Ahmed interrupted and volunteered that his wife was on the third floor, waiting for him. The hostess pointed him to the stairs. Slightly winded from the climb up the steep spiral staircase, Ahmed emerged from the stairs and surveyed the crowded third-floor dining room for Raghad. He spotted his Iraqi contact in the last table along the windows. He walked directly to her, gave her a peck on the cheek and slid into the seat across the table. Raghad acknowledged Ahmed and turned her attention back to the baby she was feeding in the high chair to her left.

Forcing a smile, Ahmed reached across the table and placed an affectionate hand on the baby's head in greeting. The waiter came over, and although Ahmed had no appetite, he ordered a hamburger and a liter of Leffe Blonde Beer. The window seat had an excellent view of the entire square. Ahmed estimated the crowd at over six hundred in the confined twenty thousand square feet of space. His pulse was racing, and he began to sweat. His beer arrived, and he gulped it down and ordered a second potent Belgian Beer. When his glass was empty, he nodded to Raghad and reached down under the table to retrieve a heavy diaper bag. He struggled sliding the heavy bag across the wooden floor.

Leaving it concealed under the table, Ahmed opened the bag. His practiced hands found the safe to arm switch by feel, and he moved it forward into the arm position. Pulling the bag out from under the table, he slid out of the booth and walked away from Raghad and her baby with the heavy diaper bag on his shoulder.

Ahmed could feel Raghad's eyes bearing down on him as he emerged from the restaurant and navigated his way through the heavy crowd toward the stage. He expected Raghad would wait until he was near the stage, where the densest cluster of people could be found, before triggering the explosive device. He could tell from people's reactions that they were starting to notice the growing panic that was reflected on his face. No longer able to feign calm, Ahmed began to hurry, crashing into people as he scurried toward the stage.

With her baby in her arms and a remote control designed to look like a baby toy in her hand, Raghad watched Ahmed through a window. Seeing Ahmed's panic, she ducked behind a nearby support pillar and triggered the device. Twenty meters from the stage, all six daisy-chained claymore mines, arrayed in a horseshoe inside the diaper bag, exploded. Each claymore, containing one and a half pounds of C4 explosive, launched seven hundred steel balls into the crowd with lethal force. In seconds, every person in the tiny square went from vertical to horizontal. The concussive force trapped inside the square shattered the windows of the Hard Rock Café and all of the surrounding buildings.

Raghad reappeared from the protection of the pillar to witness the devastation. The flying glass had lacerated the exposed and thinly covered skin of the people sitting closest to the windows. Screams and cries for help filled the restaurant.

Worst hit were the Earth Day protestors who had been gathered around the stage moments before. The activists inadvertently served as human shields as they absorbed the brunt of the lethal projectiles before they could reach the larger crowd. A Chinese tourist group was killed in its entirety when the focused spray from a single claymore hit them head-on while they were lining up for a picture.

The damage done by the blast was grotesque. In the first fifty meters fanning out from the stage, few of the bodies remained intact. It was a macabre sight of blood and dismembered bodies. When the last fatality was recorded nine days after the attack, the death toll would reach 174, with another 269 wounded.

Chapter 2

New York City

Michael Genovese felt the familiar burning in his lungs as he once again ratcheted up the pace. His target was less than a hundred yards in front of him, running with a steady, even gait that was deceptively fast.

Michael ran the same six-mile Central Park loop every day. At thirty-eight, he kept himself at the same peak level of fitness he had enjoyed while playing point guard on the basketball team at Harvard. The man he was chasing had passed him two miles back, and now his only goal in life was to retake the lead before his route ended.

His narrowing vision registered the Strawberry Fields marker off to his left, meaning he had less than a mile left to make his move. Michael took great pride in never having allowed anyone to beat him on his daily run. The pain intensified as he nudged the pace. With only a quarter mile to the finish point, he pushed it even harder. His legs were on fire, and there was a searing pain in his lungs. He could feel his vision narrow further as he forced his breathing and pumped his oxygen-deprived legs.

When he closed to within twenty yards of the interloper, he noticed it was a younger man in his twenties. The runner was oblivious to Michael as he effortlessly glided along the course, listening to music through his earbuds. Michael's breath grew even more ragged, and he was saturated in sweat as he transitioned into a full sprint for the last hundred meters to the imaginary finish line.

Barely passing the runner in the last few feet before reaching the end of the course, Michael slowed to a walk and ducked off the trail before falling to his knees. It was a full ten minutes before he was recovered enough to stand and make his way back to his apartment. Tired, but euphoric from his victory, a triumphant Michael gingerly walked across the street and made his way into the private elevator that delivered him to his penthouse apartment.

The elevator opened into a large open foyer. When the doors slid open, the first thing that met his eye was Katrina, sitting on a bench along the side of the entryway. Her bottom lip was swollen and red, and she had a large purple welt on her left cheek. Surprised to see Michael, the skittish Ukrainian withdrew from the foyer and moved behind a couch in the living room. Michael ignored the willowy young blonde and stepped around her two suitcases on his way through the living room to the hallway that led to his bedroom. He made a mental note to contact his personal assistant and request a replacement.

Despite his money and good looks, Michael's penchant for rough play with the ladies had earned him a certain notoriety within his social circles. An unfortunate dating incident with a fiercely resistant actress who happened to maintain an enormous social media network had made him radioactive to the local ladies. That event had spurred him to get creative and discover a website that advertised itself as matching "sugar babies" with "sugar daddies." Michael found that for a nominal fee, he could import some of the most beautiful and willing creatures in the world directly to his doorstep.

When he'd started to find the constant internet searching and endless chatting and messaging needed to ensnare the prospective sugar babies to be time consuming and tedious, he'd pioneered a way to outsource the work. He'd expanded on the information age mail-order concept by hiring a virtual personal assistant from India.

Shahab's daily responsibilities included uploading and managing Michael's profile on several relevant websites. His virtual PA also had the use of a shared WhatsApp messaging account and a shared email account to line up girls for delivery on demand. Michael considered his unique outsourcing method of acquiring mail-order girls to be a textbook case study in optimizing efficiencies through offshoring. Once he'd gotten his system going, he found he had created a pipeline of beautiful girls who not only bolstered his image at social events, but also accommodated his carnal needs. It was pure genius.

On his way to the shower, Michael caught his reflection in the mirror array inside the master bathroom and had to stop. He removed his clothes and posed in different positions as he flexed his well-defined muscles. With the classic Italian good looks of a young Tony Bennett, Michael never tired of studying his reflection. His rigid diet and exercise regimen were rewarded with a single-digit body fat percentage. His six-pack abdominals were his pride and joy and the focus of his gaze. As he flexed with his hands clasped in front of him in what bodybuilders referred to as the crab pose, he thought back to last night with Katrina and he swelled with pride.

After showering, Michael drove to Long Island to have lunch with his brothers. The family home was a twenty-two-thousand-square-foot estate that had been built by his father in 1969. His grandfather, Vito Genovese, had been the Don of the Genovese Crime Family until his arrest in 1957. With roots tracing back to Lucky Luciano in the 1930s, the Genovese family was sometimes referred to as the Ivy League Mafia.

After Benny "Squint" Lombardo had taken the reins following Michael's grandfather's death in prison, Michael's father, Salvatore, had used his sizable inheritance to concentrate on enterprises other than the family staples of loan sharking, drugs, gambling, prostitution and protection. At the beginning of the Vietnam War, a prescient Salvatore Genovese had invested in defense companies. He'd sent his three sons, Gino, Michael and Louis, to the best prep schools and the best colleges. Gino had attended Fordham, Michael, the scholar-athlete, had studied at Harvard, and Louis had gone to Columbia. After graduating from college, the three sons had worked with their dad and, by the mid-1990s they had assembled a strong portfolio of minority positions within the defense industry.

After Salvatore had succumbed to cancer in 1999, the three brothers had worked to secure majority shareholding positions and to unify their defense portfolio under a single management team. G3 Defense had been founded in 1999, and by 2017, the company had revenues exceeding seventeen billion dollars, twenty-seven thousand employees, and sixteen fully owned subsidiaries. In only eighteen years, G3 had become one of the largest defense firms in the United States.

Despite being the middle son, Michael was the chairman and CEO. Gino served as CFO, and Louis was the COO. The board of directors included the three brothers plus the external financiers, which included two private equity firms and Nicky Terranova, the second cousin of Barney Bellomo, the current head of the Genovese mob.

The family estate was Gino's birthright as the oldest son. He and his wife graciously hosted the extended family gathering every Sunday. Gino and Louis were both married and had five young children between them. Michael, the bachelor was a favorite uncle and despite his birth order a patriarchal figure within the family.

Michael parked his Mercedes behind Louis's Range Rover in the driveway. He was barely out of the car before being swarmed by three of his nephews, Louis, Joey, and Danny. The boys moved as a pack, attempting to submit their uncle, imitating moves learned from televised wrestling and UFC MMA. After fifteen minutes of roughhousing, he declared a draw and the joyful boys allowed a disheveled and grass-stained Michael to continue on his way to the main house.

He was met at the door by Gino's wife, Stephanie, who greeted him with a hug.

"Why do you encourage them, Michael? They ruined your good shirt."

"I don't care about the shirt. It's how boys play, Steph," said Michael.

"One of these days, they're going to hurt you."

"I think I have a few years left when I can handle them," said Michael as Stephanie led him into the kitchen by the arm.

After dinner, the three brothers retired to the home theater to watch the Yankees play the Orioles. The brothers were seated in leather recliners, drinking beer in front of an eighty-inch plasma TV and waiting for the start of the game.

"Have you been following the news about what's going on in Belgium?" Michael asked.

"Yes, that was terrible. Those Europeans need to get serious about those immigrants," said Gino.

"I bet we see a spike in our Security and Detection revenues. Nobody sells body scanners better than those jihadis," Louis said.

"That's not the only good that'll come of it. That guy from Abu Dhabi isn't going to be a problem anymore," Michael said.

"What guy in Abu Dhabi? What are you talking about, Michael?" said Gino.

"Nothing… just that I heard a rumor about that guy who was digging into our business a while back. Seems he might have some bigger things to worry about," Michael said. Gino and Louis looked at each other with puzzled expressions and then switched the subject back to the NBA Playoffs.

Chapter 3

Eleuthera, Bahamas

Pat straddled his surfboard and positioned himself so that he could watch the incoming swells over his right shoulder and see the beach over his left shoulder. It was a sunny spring day. The rolling waves were turquoise until they broke into a white foam and raced onto the blushing pink strip of sand.

Beyond the beach, Pat could see the top floors of his beach house peeking above the gently swaying palms. He shifted his gaze downward and surveyed the surf line, looking for Diane. He spotted her in a sea of white, working her way out through the surf. Every seven seconds she would vanish under an incoming wave and then reappear without missing a stroke. She moved fast, with the grace and power of an elite athlete. Diane smiled as she reached Pat. It was a dazzling smile accompanied by emerald-green eyes set in a stunningly beautiful face.

"Are you a tourist or a surfer?" asked Diane.

"I'm enjoying the view while I wait for the perfect wave."

"The tide's starting to go out, and it's only going to get worse. You better take what you can get."

"Yeah, you're right. One last wave, then it's time for lunch."

Pat and Diane carried their surfboards under opposite arms as they walked to the house. Between the beach and the house was a narrow trail encroached by lush ground vegetation. The two threaded their way through the narrow trail, past the guesthouse and the pool house until they reached the main house, a three-story peach-colored stone mansion with eight bedrooms.

Pat had been staying at the beach house for almost five months, and the daily surfing and regular workout routine had him in better shape than he had been in a long time. The beach house was his retirement dream home, everything in it built to his specifications. The second-floor deck was his favorite spot, offering a view of the Atlantic Ocean to the east and the Caribbean to the west.

Diane was a surfer girl from Florida. The two had met a year ago when she was waitressing at Tippy's, the neighboring beachfront restaurant where he was a regular customer. Over a period of months, the relationship had progressed from customer and waitress to surf student and surfing guru, and then to soulmates. Pat was head over heels in love with Diane, and for the past three months, the two had lived a honeymoon existence at the beach house.

Pat was just stepping out of the shower when he received a call from Jessica, his office manager. The Trident headquarters were located three miles up island in Governor's Harbour. Trident was a CIA subcontractor that had a single contract with the US government to supply military goods to US allied forces in Syria and Iraq.

Pat answered the call, and before he could even say hello, a panicked Jessica interrupted.

"We have a serious problem."

"What's going on?"

"All of our bank accounts have been frozen, and our export license requests, purchase orders and payments have been put on hold by the government contract office," said Jessica.

"Any idea why?"

"They didn't even give me notice. I was trying to transfer money from the CITI account online and it rejected every transaction. I tried the same with the accounts in the Bahamas and got the same thing. Then I received a notice from DCMA that our contract is suspended, still with no explanation."

"Give me a few minutes to make some calls, and I'll get back to you," said Pat.

Using the secure app on his CIA-issued smartphone, Pat called Mike Guthrie, a friend from his days as a junior officer in the Second Ranger Battalion. The two had gone their separate ways after Delta selection and had been reunited seventeen years later in Afghanistan, when Mike was a CIA agent and Pat was a down-on-his-luck defense contractor working as a military advisor to the Afghan National Army. Mike had recruited Pat as an asset, and the two had been working together professionally for last five years. Mike was currently assigned to Langley in the Clandestine Operations Directorate, while Pat's company, Trident, was part of a black operation that was managed by the Department of Defense. Trident was the conduit for military supplies to the Peshmerga and other forces fighting against ISIS in Syria and Iraq.

When, after ten rings, Mike did not pick up, Pat terminated the call. He looked across the table to Dianne. "I don't have time to explain this. Just pack a bag. We need to be out of here in five minutes."

Pat stood from his chair at the kitchen table and sprinted up the stairs toward his office on the third floor. He quickly opened his safe and removed two packages. One held passports for both him and Diane, and the second contained cash and cell phone SIM cards. Next, he went into a storage closet and withdrew a duffle bag. With the bag filled, he ran downstairs and entered the garage through the kitchen entrance, throwing the heavy black nylon duffel bag into the back of the Tahoe.

Diane entered the garage a few seconds later, and they both jumped into the Tahoe and sped off.

Less than a mile away, on the Caribbean side of the island, was a small marina that was home to a small local fishing fleet. The sole recreational vehicle in the marina was Pat's sixty-four-foot motor yacht. The Azimut 64 Flybridge had been his home for three years when he'd lived in Abu Dhabi, United Arab Emirates. Since his relocation to the Bahamas, beyond the occasional fishing trip or quick day trip to Nassau, the boat had largely been ignored.

Pat detached the external power connection and untied the boat from the slip while Diane went to the wheelhouse and started the twin Caterpillar 1150-horsepower engines. Runway Cove Marina had a very narrow access point designed for the smaller fishing vessels. Navigating the narrow passage and the sharp dogleg turn was a tricky maneuver that would have been impossible without the bow thrusters. Once through the gap and into the Caribbean, Pat gradually increased the speed to twenty-eight knots and set a heading for Nassau, fifty miles to the west.

Diane approached Pat while he was sitting at the helm station on the flybridge.

"What's going on?" asked Diane.

"Honestly, honey, I have no idea. All I know is that the US government has suspended my IDIQ contract, and all of my business and personal bank accounts have been frozen," said Pat.

"Are you in trouble with the IRS or something?" said Diane.

"You've seen the scars on my body, and you have a general idea of what I used to do for a living. The government contracts Trident supports are so sensitive I'm not even allowed to discuss them, but they're essential to US policy, and they aren't something that can be casually suspended without serious cause," said Pat.

"So, what does that mean?" said Diane.

"It means anything big enough to cause the government to shut down my business operations is serious enough to make me want to disappear until I can get ahold of the people I work for and figure out what the hell is going on," said Pat.

"Are we in danger?"

"I don't think so. When the US government freezes your bank accounts and cuts off a contract that's strategically important, it must mean an arrest is soon to follow. The only reason I didn't leave you at the house is that I don't know who's after me."

"Why would the US government arrest you?" said Diane.

"I haven't done anything wrong that I know of, but having my money and my business contracts frozen and my contact in the CIA unavailable has me spooked," said Pat.

"Now I'm scared."

"Throw your phone overboard. We need to remain unfindable until I can figure this thing out," said Pat.

It took almost two hours to sail to Nassau Harbor. Diane was clingy for most of the trip, and while Pat would have preferred to spend the time planning, instead he'd found himself responding to an endless stream of questions and concerns from Diane. During the few respites from her desire to be assured, he'd quietly debated whether it would be safer to drop Diane off in Nassau. Ultimately, he'd decided to keep her with him. Partly out of selfishness, since he couldn't stand to be away from her, and partly because he knew it would cause her just as much pain for her to be away from him. It was poor operational reasoning, and he hoped he wouldn't regret it.

Pat docked at a transient slip in the Palm Cay Marina. Unlike his tiny fishing marina in Governor's Harbour, the Palm Cay was built for luxury tourism, and with one hundred and ninety-five mostly occupied slips, his yacht blended in perfectly. Pat booked for two days and paid the docking fee of two dollars per foot per day to the harbormaster. Once they had the power and water connected, they locked up the boat and walked to the car rental office located inside the marina clubhouse.

"What's next?" asked Diane.

"We need to provision the boat with food for a three-week journey. There's a Fresh Market a few miles from here that should have everything we need. We also need lunch, and I need to find Wi-Fi so I can contact my people. Once we load up and prep the boat, we'll fill the external fuel tanks. That'll give us a range of close to three thousand miles and then we'll be ready to depart tomorrow morning," said Pat.

"Depart for where?"

"At this point, it's more about getting off the grid. I really don't have any particular destination in mind."

"That doesn't sound like much of a plan," Diane said with a smile. Pat put his arm around Diane and kissed the top of her head.

"It's not, but if it turns out I have to be on the run, we might as well make a holiday of it."

The first stop was lunch. Still unwilling to put a cell phone in operation, Pat used the navigation system on the rental car and settled on a nearby restaurant called Luciano of Chicago. It was almost three in the afternoon, and the restaurant was nearly empty. While he was waiting for his shrimp and scallop ceviche appetizer, Pat turned on his laptop and connected to the restaurant's free Wi-Fi. Using a TOR app, he was able to mask his IP address and location and encrypt his communications. He went on Google Messenger and sent a message to Mike Guthrie.

"The contract has been suspended and all my personal and business accounts are frozen. What gives?" he wrote.

After devouring a magnificent seven-ounce filet mignon with asparagus and mashed potatoes, he received a reply from Mike.

"Explosives used in Brussels bombing originated from Trident. JTTF has identified you as a subject of the investigation, and an arrest order has been issued," Mike replied.

"Does the JTTF know what I do and who I work for?" wrote Pat.

"No. The director wants to avoid a scandal. The case against you is strong and getting stronger. Disappear and give me some time to find out who's pulling the strings on this," Mike replied.

"Done, will check back with you daily on this channel."

"Any updates you want to share?" Diane asked. Pat sipped his double espresso while looking across the table at Diane's concerned expression.

"The good news is that there's no physical danger. The bad news is as I suspected. I need to disappear while the people I work for clear this problem up."

"What do you mean by disappear?"

"It means we spend a few weeks on the Atlantic, looking for the perfect wave," Pat said.

Diane smiled. "Being on the run with you sounds like fun."

Chapter 4

San Sebastian, Spain

Pat was seated at a small table in the far back of the Bar Nestor restaurant. He felt fortunate to have already been served a beer by the overworked waitress. He and Diane had sailed into the town of San Sebastian four days earlier. Located deep in Basque Country in the north of Spain, the picturesque harbor town was renowned for its indulgences. Recognized as a global gastronomical destination, San Sebastian was also home to Playa de la Zurriola, one of the best surfing beaches on the planet. The combination was irresistible to Pat and Diane, and the quaint nineteenth-century architecture, friendly people and beautiful rolling green hills surrounding the harbor were an added bonus.

It had been two weeks since they'd departed the Bahamas in the *Sam Houston*. The Atlantic crossing had been uneventful, with good weather and calm seas. They stopped on the way for some island hopping in the Azures, the Canary Islands and Ibiza. When they'd arrived at San Sebastian, they'd docked the yacht in the local marina and settled into a routine of surfing and exploring the molecular gastro dining that San Sebastian was famous for.

The restaurant was narrow, with a long wooden bar that extended the full length of the room on one side. Small tables and big windows lined the wall across from the bar. The walls and even the ceiling were covered with framed sports memorabilia, mostly jerseys from local football players. The tiny bar was overcrowded, with people lined up two and three deep. Pat was forced to fend off several covetous denizens trying to snag the lone empty chair across from his small table. With slight irritation, he found himself twice having to remind an overly persistent heavyset woman that the chair was taken. Mike Guthrie surprised him when he emerged from behind the woman's sizable girth with a magician's flourish. Pat stood and embraced his old friend.

"This is a bit too crowded for our purposes, don't you think?" Mike said.

"The minimum wait for a reservation is three days. When I made the reservation, I had a different dinner companion in mind," Pat said.

"Sticking to your old reservation was a good call. It would make it hard to surveil you unless someone knew where you were going to be three days ago."

"We should stay. The food's supposed to be amazing. They have only three items on the menu, and foodies from all over the world come here and refer to the three dishes as the holy trinity. This place has a cult following," Pat said.

"That's a lot to live up to. What are the items?"

"Wait and see, it won't be long." Pat ordered two pints of the local craft beer, which had the unfortunate name of Gross, just as the first course of the trinity was arriving.

"According to my tourist guidebook, tomato salad, or *corazón de buey*, consists of oxheart tomatoes that have been splashed with rich olive oil and just a little white wine vinegar. Then they're doused with salt and served with hunks of crusty bread," said Pat.

The harried waitress dropped a large white plate the size of a pizza on their table and hurriedly moved along. Minutes later, she muscled her way back through the crowd with the second menu item: a heaping plate of fried padron peppers. The large green chilis had been flash-fried in a hot pan with a little olive oil. The two men switched from beer to goblet-sized glasses of gin and tonic.

"The next course is the crowning glory. It's called the txuleta. A txuleta is a Basque cut of beef so big that it could have been hacked off a dinosaur. It's a sirloin on the bone, two pounds f meat that's been cooked slowly over hot coals before being sliced, then doused with salt and served. No accompaniments. No side dishes. Just a juicy, salty, perfectly cooked steak of Flintstone proportion," said Pat.

"Caveman food," said Mike.

"Exactly, which is why I'm glad you're here and not Diane. She wouldn't enjoy it half as much."

Moments later, the waitress returned with two huge steaks that were straining her arms. They were served on a black iron plate resting on a slab of wood. Liberally sprinkled on the steak and plate were white chunks of sea salt. The rough wooden table clanged when she ceremoniously landed the heavy cargo. For the next thirty minutes, the two men were silent.

"That's the single best meal I've ever eaten. Tomatoes, bread, peppers and steak. Pretty basic stuff, but cooked perfectly," said Mike.

"It didn't just live up to its billing, it exceeded it."

"Is this what you've been up to, eating yourself across the planet?"

"Pretty much. This town has the highest density of Michelin-rated restaurants in the world. Diane and I surf during the day and dedicate our nights to culinary pursuits. It turns out that being an international fugitive on the run heightens my appetite. Something about never knowing which day is going to be your last makes you appreciate the moment all that much more," Pat said.

"That's a legitimate concern."

"I thought you would have sorted this misunderstanding out by now," said Pat.

The small dining room was beginning to clear. Mike turned around to make sure none of the other patrons were within earshot before continuing the conversation.

"When the Joint Terrorism Task Force wasn't able to clear you with its own investigation, we went ahead and gave them enough exculpatory information to make the problem go away. We informed them that you were a CIA asset and provided many of the details of your operation. JTTF went to the attorney general's office and requested a lifting of the arrest order and recommended a removal of the lock on your assets.

"OFAC, the Office of Financial Asset Control, is an independent organization, and based on the weight of the case file, they just went ahead and cleared you and unlocked your accounts. But the attorney general dissented at the recommendation of the JTTF. The attorney general's office has maintained the order for your arrest."

"That makes no sense," said Pat.

"I know."

"The explosives used were received by Trident for delivery to the Peshmerga. How they got to Belgium and into the possession of an ISIS terrorist is a mystery to everyone. There's no evidence to suggest Trident didn't deliver the shipment to the Peshmerga, and once it left Trident's control, how could we be held responsible? How could they accuse me without any proof? This is ridiculous. There's nothing to incriminate me."

"That's the sixty-four-thousand-dollar question. Somebody's out to get you," Mike said.

"I agree, but why do you say it?"

"Simple. JTTF took you off the chopping block, and the AG put you back on."

"I don't even know who the AG is—why would he go after me?" said Pat.

"It might not be the AG himself. He may be responding to pressure from someone else, or it might be an underling," Mike said.

"Do you think this is related to the Prince Bandar tapes?"

"It seems likely. This might actually be a break. We suspected there were elements within the US government who were sabotaging that operation. It could be they found an opportunity to retaliate by putting you out of business and took it."

"I'm having trouble seeing how putting Trident out of business benefits anyone in the US government," Pat said.

"I don't know the answer to that either. All we know is that someone is seriously fucking with you. They have shown themselves, and now for the first time we have something to work with."

"Catching government employees subverting a CIA black operation isn't exactly my skill set," said Pat.

"I'd agree with that," said Mike.

"What happens next?"

"You killed three sheiks who were financing ISIS last year. Prince Bandar indicated possible American support when you interrogated him. We had an element within the State Department move to suppress Bandar's interrogation. It might be that, after laying low for a while, they think it's a good time to make another move," said Mike.

"What does anybody gain by shutting Trident down and locking me up? I gave everything I have to the Agency months ago. There's nothing left to come out."

"It's either retaliation for the past or a move to stop you from interfering in the future. But like I said, it's a good thing, because now we may have a lead. You can't interfere with JTTF investigators without leaving fingerprints. Influencing the investigation is a huge risk, and I don't believe anyone would take on a risk that great simply for revenge," said Mike.

"So, where does that leave us?"

"The Trident operation and you specifically are somehow a problem to whoever's doing this. We need to make sure you remain a problem," Mike said.

"What do you have in mind?"

Two fresh gin and tonics were delivered to the table. The restaurant was half-empty now, and the noise level was slightly louder from the satisfied diners.

"The deputy director of clandestine operations wants Trident back in business. The plan is to use you as bait."

Pat smiled. "I buy you the best meal of your life, and your repayment is to dangle me in front of the bad guys."

"We're going to move the funding of Trident from DOD to a more clandestine route within the Agency. With Mosul mostly secured and Raqqa ready to fall, the DOD orders would have slowed anyway. Most of the work now is in Africa. The arrest order against you is going to remain. We got your assets released, but I'm sure the FISA court has authorized a full sweep on all of your communications. Getting around will be a little difficult for you. Make sure you stay out of the US," said Mike.

"Who's on our team?"

"Me and my department, obviously. The DDCO, the CIA director and the president," Mike said.

"The president? Does he even know I exist?"

"I went with the director to brief him and he was pissed. I showed the president your service record and told him about what you did last year. We have the top cover we need to root this thing out," said Mike.

"Find them and kill them—finally, a plan I can work with." Pat grinned.

"Get back to Abu Dhabi and press on with your operations. But before that, make sure you pay the tab and leave that nice waitress a big tip," said Mike.

"All I am to you is an ATM and bait on a hook."

"How were you able to keep the business going after the feds put a freeze on everything?"

"I've learned a few things from you over the years. I have IDs, weapons and small amounts of cash strategically stashed around the world. I also had a fair amount of money in bitcoin that was part of a speculative position I've been experimenting with. In the last six months, the value of bitcoin has tripled. I have absolutely no idea why, but it came in handy."

"That's risky. The computer guys at the NSA are better than you think. Anything on the internet is going to be caught and forwarded to the investigators, especially if you have a FISA warrant against you," said Mike.

"The thing with these digital currencies is that you don't have to leave your money in someone else's computer or use the internet. You can retain them on your own hardware. Each bitcoin is a distinct line of code that can be exchanged for currency, and you can carry them around with you. I have a drive the size of a lighter that has over twenty million dollars in it."

"How do you convert it to currency? That's when they'll catch you," Mike said.

"There are exchanges, both physical and internet based. I've been making payroll and keeping a couple of pretty expensive airplanes in the air using these distinctive lines of code," Pat said. "If the US government has a way to monitor and regulate the bitcoin market, I'm definitely not seeing it."

"Well, you shouldn't have to worry about using bitcoins anymore. You now have access to your normal banking channels. When you get to Abu Dhabi, track down the chain of custody on those explosives. It would be good to know where and how that shipment got diverted. It'll also help to make that arrest order disappear."

"Amen to that," Pat said.

Chapter 5

Washington, D.C.

Michael Genovese wheeled his black Mercedes S65L through the iron gate and onto the brick driveway. His legs were cramped and his back was stiff from driving four hours without a break from New York City to Palisades, D.C. The navigation system had predicted the trip would take over five hours, but Michael hadn't bought a twelve-cylinder performance car for no reason.

The driveway meandered through a wooded grove, and the house came into view behind a huge oak tree. He wheeled around a circular driveway that was dominated by a large Roman fountain in the center. Lucian Rossi was standing like a valet on the front porch between two of the tall white columns that lined the front of the manor. Michael brought the car to a halt in front of the entryway. Lucian Rossi, the senior senator from Connecticut, descended the stairs and greeted Michael.

"How was the drive?"

"I made good time, traffic was light. I like the new place. What did this run you?" Michael said.

"I got a great deal. It was seven and a half million. You want to take the nickel tour?" Lucian grasped Michael's arm above the elbow to guide him, but Michael shook him off.

Lucian was animated as he walked Michael through the house. It was a well-rehearsed script and included many amusing anecdotes. The tour ended in the billiard room. The room had three areas—a section with a professional-grade pool table, an ornate wooden bar with a mahogany countertop, and a sitting area next to the picture windows overlooking the pool.

"I like what you've done with this room. The dark tones, oak and leather remind me of the Harvard Club in Boston."

"That's what I was aiming for. This is where I like to spend most of my quality time."

The Genoveses and Rossis were two Italian-American families with very different stories. Lucian's father had been the governor of Connecticut and an advisor to three presidents, and his grandfather had served on the Supreme Court. Lucian's great-grandfather had been a hard-scrabble Italian immigrant who'd made a fortune in construction and real estate at the beginning of the twentieth century. The family had lived grandly on that fortune until the fateful day they learned their close family friend, Barry Madoff, had made the Rossi family trust disappear. In 2010, Lucian's reelection as senator had been in grave danger. The combination of a Tea Party challenge and an emerging scandal involving underage girls at a hedge fund owner's private island had threatened to unseat him. With his finances in ruins and his political future in jeopardy, Lucian was, for the first time in his life, facing the stark reality of having to toil in the dreaded private sector to survive. Always on the lookout for opportunities, Michael had learned of Lucian's predicament and made him an offer.

Lucian had been thirteen points behind in the polls on Labor Day. At that time, he was isolated, ostracized and cast out from the party establishment. The chairwoman of the Democrat National Committee had refused to take his calls, and his pleas for campaign cash and support had been ignored for months. Lucian's political death spiral had reversed when the Republican challenger had unexpectedly dropped out of the race in mid-October. The tragic death of the challenger's seventeen-year-old daughter from a drug overdose had devastated the man and caused him to completely withdraw from public life.

Lucian had eventually cruised to victory against an obscure last-minute backup candidate. With his political and financial fortunes miraculously restored, Lucian had worked hard to repair his reputation. He had handily won his most recent reelection. The mysterious drug overdose of a vibrant seventeen-year-old National Merit Scholar whose friends insisted never took a drink of alcohol had been life-changing for Lucian. It was also part of a devil's bargain he could never escape.

Lucian poured a sparkling water for Michael and a double scotch and soda for himself.

"This is a terrific place," said Michael.

"Emma and I really enjoy it."

"I can see why you didn't return to Connecticut for the recess."

"The bigger reason is too much work, I have a busy travel schedule planned."

"Is that with the Armed Services Committee or the Intelligence Committee?"

"Both. I leave next week for Europe. I'll be visiting London, Paris and Berlin," said Lucian.

"Beyond taxpayer-funded summer holidays, what's the Armed Services and Intelligence Committees doing about protecting the country from the threat of Pat Walsh?"

"What do you mean?" Lucian asked.

"Why did you let him off the hook? I'm being told he's back in business."

"He was completely cleared by the JTTF investigation. The recommendation was to drop everything and reinstate him completely. I had to use some serious pull to force DOD to maintain the suspend order on Trident's IDIQ contract. The only reason he still has a warrant out for his arrest is because of my efforts," Lucian said.

"That's not good enough. The State Department is still approving his export licenses, and all the business he had with DOD is now going through the CIA. You need to put the freeze back onto his assets. He's a major threat," Michael said.

"I don't think he's a threat to anything. He's just a gun dealer. One of many that the US government contracts to support the global war on terror," Lucian said.

"Unless we destroy this guy, both he and his buddy in the CIA are going to continue to dig around. He came very close last year to bringing the entire operation down. I set him up, all you had to do was to make sure the government agencies finished him. Those agencies depend on you for funding—why is that hard?" Michael asked.

"When I pushed to override the reinstate order, I drew a lot of attention and made a lot of people suspicious. I cannot put any more pressure on Walsh without risking exposure and compromising everything."

"I need you to maintain the pressure on Walsh. The man is a fugitive. How the hell can the US government do business with a fugitive? Everything he has should be seized, his contracts should be terminated and he should be hunted down and arrested," said Michael.

"The case against Walsh is beyond weak. It's practically nonexistent. The only proof is that the bombing was done with explosives that at one time passed through his company. No motive, no proof he redirected the shipment. It was a routine transaction. As far as we know Walsh was never even aware of the shipment. The only reason Walsh is still a subject of the investigation with an arrest warrant and sanctions is because of me. The problem is, I'm overplaying my hand on this, and people are wondering why I'm interfering. If I keep pushing this, it's going to lead Walsh to me and then to you. You saw what he did to Bandar and those two sheiks—you need to be careful of Walsh."

Michael caught himself before his temper flared out of control. In a soft, controlled voice, he replied, "I don't need to be careful of anyone, especially Walsh. He needs to be careful of me. I got to where I'm at today by destroying my enemies, not by hiding from them. Remember who pays for this good life, Mr. Senator," Michael said.

"We have a crazy reality TV star for a president who wants to withdraw our military forces from around the world, which would not only destroy the country, but also ruin my business. That isn't going to happen, I promise you. I'm going to teach that real estate salesman that the world is a dangerous place and that if you don't go to the enemy, the enemy will come to you. Anyone who gets in the way of that lesson is going to pay a price. That includes Walsh, and it also includes you, Senator. I suggest you climb back on board, because I don't like your attitude."

Lucian could feel his knees shaking as he stood to walk Michael out the door. He couldn't wait to usher the demon out of his sanctuary and return to the comfort and warmth of the Johnnie Walker Blue in his billiard room.

With the city traffic, it took Michael thirty-five minutes to reach the K Street Brownstone office of TSG Consulting. Richard Silver, the CEO of The Silver Group, had had an illustrious twenty-two-year career as a senator from Georgia before serving as secretary of defense. After leaving public service, he had founded one of the preeminent lobbying firms specializing in the defense industry.

Michael was ushered into the plush office by a fresh-faced twenty-something intern. The TSG CEO had the looks, the mannerisms and the grand office needed to project the distinguished statesman and D.C. powerbroker vibe. Silver made it look effortless, but Michael was sure it was carefully cultivated.

"Good to see you, Michael, you look terrific. How much time to do you have?"

"I have a couple of hours," Michael said.

"The Littoral Combat Ship settlement has been accepted by DOD. G3 is going to be awarded five hundred and forty million to make the software upgrades and design changes to the propulsion and fire control systems," Silver said.

"What about the next order?"

"The Navy wants to stick to just the eight systems. They're in negotiations with General Dynamics for a firm fixed price award for twelve frigates."

"We need to change that," said Michael.

"That isn't going to be easy. There's a lot of dissatisfaction with the LCS program. The Navy gave G3 three point two billion to build eight ships that don't work, and now they've approved another half a billion to repair them. It's unlikely they're going to repeat."

"It's a first-in-its-class program—a few glitches and minor cost overruns are to be expected," Michael said.

"The Navy wants the more reliable frigates."

"We need to change their mind. This is a five-billion-dollar deal that's at stake. What can we do?"

"GD still hasn't fixed the launch problem with the new Ford-class carrier. That and the cost overruns that brought the tab to thirteen billion are enough justification for Lucian to put a hold on awarding another major ship-building contract to GD while a review takes place. The LCS is a better ship, and the cost is the same. We just need time to help the right people understand the benefit," said Silver.

"What kind of budget are you going to need to win this?"

"A hundred and fifty million, offshore," said Silver.

"I'll arrange it today. But first, give me the details of the plan."

Hours later, Michael entered the onramp to I-95 and headed north to New York City. He weaved through traffic at a steady ninety miles per hour, listening only to the powerful growl of the 600cc engine. The meeting with TSG had been a success; Richard Silver had a can-do attitude. The meeting with Lucian nagged at him, though; he hated quitters. He tried to fantasize about what he was going to do with Vanya, the pretty Bulgarian girl he'd had flown in yesterday, but his mind kept returning to Lucian's warning to stay away from Walsh. The insolence of the senator still rankled him. Michael hadn't gotten to where he was by backing away from government flunkies and small-time gun runners.

Chapter 6

Abu Dhabi, UAE

Sweat stung his eyes and blurred his vision as Pat manipulated the joystick control station on the aft deck of the yacht. He gently backed the sixty-four-foot yacht into the narrow slip, and Diane tossed the line to a waiting dock worker, a dark-skinned Indian laborer who appeared undaunted by the blazing August heat. The laborer scrambled to catch the short toss and expertly secured the line before moving on to the next.

"Is that where we're staying?" Diane asked, pointing.

"It's the Emirates Palace Hotel. I hope you don't think it's too stuffy," said Pat.

"It's huge, it looks like a real palace."

"If you look to the west, you can see the Presidential Palace. The two buildings don't look all that different," Pat said.

"It's a short walk from the marina—that's going to make checking in easier."

"Yeah, I got a suite on the first floor on the West Wing side. You can walk directly to the beach, the pool and the marina."

"In this heat, don't expect me to spend much time outside," Diane said.

"Early morning and after sundown are the only times to be outside this time of year."

"After three months on a boat with surf stops in Spain, Morocco, Senegal, South Africa and the Maldives, I think a couple days indoors in a hotel is perfect," said Diane.

"Let's get the boat cleaned up first, then we can hang out with the beautiful people," Pat said.

Pat and Diane left their room and entered the labyrinth of seemingly endless Emirates Palace hallways. "You may want to take off your heels and carry them; this is going to be a long walk," said Pat.

Diane quickly switched to bare feet as they entered a major hallway.

"Let me give you the statistics on this. This place is massive. The main palace building stretches over a kilometer from wing to wing. The hotel has one hundred and fourteen domes. The big dome in the middle is more than two hundred feet high. The interior is covered with gold, pearls and crystals. The palace has over one thousand chandeliers, the largest weighing over two and a half tons. This place is the epitome of ostentatious."

As Pat was finishing his role as tour guide, they reached the entrance to the Hakkasan Restaurant. A smiling Asian hostess escorted the couple through the dimly lit restaurant, elegantly decorated with Chinese art. They could hear muted chatter from the other patrons and a harpist playing softly in the background.

It was not until they were next to the table that Pat was able to spot Muy Muy Migos and Bill Sachse. Both men stood to greet Pat, and they exchanged handshakes. Diane was introduced and the four sat down. Sachse and Migos were both drinking beer. Pat looked over the iPad wine menu and ordered a bottle of Chateau d'Yquem Lur Saluces 1999. When the waitress arrived, he also ordered a dim sum platter, duck rolls and wagyu beef ribs as starters.

"Boss, you should have told me you were bringing a date. I could have used this as an opportunity to work through the waiting list," said Migos.

"Is this the point where you explain to Diane why people call you Muy Muy?" said Pat.

"There's no need. Woman know instinctively, it's a gift," Migos replied.

Pat smiled. He had been away for months and missed the camaraderie of the team in Abu Dhabi. Trident only had thirteen employees. Three worked finance and admin from the Bahamas, and ten worked in Abu Dhabi, managing logistics and crewing the two C-130J aircraft that shuttled equipment, weapons and ammunition to whoever the US government felt needed them the most.

"So, boss, are you going to explain why we spent almost two months sitting on our asses while supplies piled up on the tarmac of the air base?" said Migos.

Pat looked across the table and noticed the laconic Sachse focus his attention for the first time of the evening. "Sure, you deserve an explanation. The terrorist explosion in Brussels back in April was conducted with claymore mines that Trident delivered to the Peshmerga more than a year ago. For some unknown reason, the investigators believe the claymores were diverted by Trident. The government conducted an investigation. They froze my assets, suspended all contracts and issued an order for my arrest."

"Is everything clear now?" said Sachse.

"It's mostly cleared up. The evidence that Trident diverted the shipment doesn't exist, but still I'm not cleared because we did take receipt and they were used by terrorists. Anyway, there are some politicians calling for my head. We're still in business because the people that matter know it's all bullshit, and they recognize what we do is important. The reason I came back out here is because I intend to conduct my own investigation to find out what happened to those claymores."

"You want to kill the guilty bastard and clear your name," said Sachse.

"If we didn't have friends in high places, we'd be out of business, and I'd be in a prison cell. The people in D.C. that stood up for me also put themselves out on a limb. For reasons that I don't understand, there are some folks trying to saw that limb off. I'm going to track that claymore shipment from where we delivered it in Iraq to where they were used in Brussels. I'm going to clear this mess up once and for all," said Pat.

"Awesome, count me in. I'll have your battle rattle ready to go first thing tomorrow morning," said Migos.

"We delivered the shipment into Sulaymaniyah Airport in January of 2016, so that's where I'll be flying to the day after tomorrow," Pat said.

"You need to bring me along. All the records are going to be in either Kurmanji or Arabic," Migos said.

"That's a good point, I agree," said Pat.

"Plus, since you always find trouble, you'll need me around to save your ass," Migos added.

"Yeah, that's the way I remember it too, getting into trouble and getting saved over and over again by Muy Muy Migos," Pat said. Even the straight-faced Sachse couldn't help but laugh.

"Let's order some main courses, get some more wine and worry about this stuff later," Pat said.

"Now we're talking," said Diane.

Later, after the pan-fried venison, wok-fried Alaskan king crab legs, grilled king prawns, sweet and sour chicken, and noodles and rice were reduced to mere remnants, Pat ordered a round of Nikka Taketsuru 21 as a nightcap. Diane and Migos were locked in an animated conversation, and although Pat could not hear it, the hand gestures and hysterical laughter from Diane were enough for him to pick up that the story involved one of Migos's many romantic adventures. Sachse sipped his Japanese whiskey cautiously.

"It's not exactly Kentucky bourbon, but I have to admit, it's drinkable," said Sachse.

"The Japanese make an excellent scotch. It's a mystery," said Pat.

"Lots of mysteries going on, from the sound of it. I have some friends at the US embassy—should I ask them to help out?" Sachse said.

"It's a long story, but based on my experience last time I was here, I'm pretty sure at least some of the folks at the embassy are playing for the other team. It's best to keep the circle small," Pat said.

As Pat was paying the bill, Migos chimed in, "Where to now, boss? You had this poor girl cooped up in a tiny boat for months with nothing to look at but your ugly face. You owe her a night out."

Pat looked at Diane, who, despite the late hour, appeared full of energy.

"Let's go next door to Etoiles and drink champagne and dance with the rich and famous," said Pat.

As the four approached the club entrance, the vibration from the bass grew steadily. When they neared the velvet rope and the superhuman-sized bouncer, Sachse touched Pat's arm.

"I'm going to call it a night. Doesn't look like there's going to be any country music playing anytime soon in that place," said Sachse.

The club was crowded and the noise of the electronic dance music was deafening. Pat purchased a VIP table and the three sat on a sofa behind a coffee table facing the smoky dance floor complete with strobe lights and dancing lasers. Pat ordered two bottles of Veuve Clicquot.

"Two bottles? Do I need to get you enrolled in a twelve-step program?" said Migos.

Pat laughed. "I'm just trying to help you out. Once the ladies see I'm with Diane, all that's left to draw them in is the champagne. I'm setting you up as a high roller. We can tell them the second Muy is for your bank account," said Pat. Migos and Diane laughed.

Migos glanced toward the dance floor. "The problem is, you've never seen Muy Muy in action. I'll be back." He slipped under the velvet VIP rope and was lost in the crowd.

Diane took Pat by the arm and led him to the dance floor. Several songs later, they returned to find the table full. Migos was with three pretty young girls of mixed nationalities, all dressed to the nines. Pat retreated to the end of the table with Diane. He ordered two more bottles of champagne and sat on the sofa, snuggling up close to Diane to watch the follies. At the peak, Migos was surrounded by a crowd of seven girls. All of them were dancing around and occasionally on the table. At one point, the bouncer had to step in to issue a warning to a Pamala Anderson lookalike who was unbuttoning Muy Muy's shirt. The tall Ukrainian bombshell had a figure that could only be achieved with synthetic enhancement, and her minuscule dress was designed to display as much as legally possible of the medical achievement. Muy Muy, the five-foot-nine Greek Adonis with the Popeye arms was clearly in his element. Diane never stopped smiling.

It was after three in the morning when they returned to their suite. Once in the room, Pat quickly undressed and hopped under the covers. The hypersexuality of the club had filled him with expectation.

When Diane returned from the bathroom, she was wearing a bathrobe and a very serious expression. "You've never fully explained to me what you do for a living," she said as she took a seat in the chair nearest to the bed.

"Do you mind if we table this conversation until tomorrow?" Pat said as he felt his highly anticipated plans begin to fade.

"No, this is a discussion I want to have now. What I learned tonight is that you're about to do something very dangerous. You always say you're in the logistics business, but I don't think you've been honest with me," said Diane.

Pat got out of the bed and walked to the mini-bar, returning with a Corona. "I own a company called Trident, which you already know. Trident supports the US government with military supplies, which again you already know. What is it you want me to explain?" Pat said.

"Sachse and Migos aren't store clerks, and what you discussed tonight wasn't exactly business talk. I'm starting to think you're some kind of mercenary or something," said Diane.

"No, we're not. The logistics services we provide to the government support the war on terror. We deliver military supplies to various countries in the Middle East and North Africa. Trident has two C-130 cargo planes that make those deliveries. Sachse is a crew chief and Migos is a crew member on one of those aircraft. Each of the cargo planes has a crew of four. One of the crews has a flight in a few hours, so they couldn't attend the dinner tonight. The two pilots on Migos and Sachse's plane had other plans, so it was just them who came out with us," Pat said.

"Tell me about this business of you playing detective in Iraq."

"The reason a warrant was issued for my arrest, and the reason my assets were frozen and Trident's contracts were suspended, was because Trident was accused of diverting military supplies to terrorists. My trip to Iraq will be to find out how the material we delivered got into the hands of the wrong people. I need Migos, because he speaks the languages of the people I need to interview."

"I thought you were cleared," Diane said.

"I was cleared by the government organization we have the contract with, but there are still accusations being made against Trident from other parts of the government. There's pressure to reinstate the penalties, and the only way to make the problem go away is to find evidence that clears me. I have to show that we delivered the goods to the right people," Pat said.

"What organization do you have a contract with?"

"The CIA."

"You and Migos and Sachse all work for the CIA. I could tell those guys weren't regular businessmen."

"Everyone in my company has a military special operations background. Mostly they're Air Force Special Operations Command. Migos and his counterpart on the other crew are from the Army Special Forces. Trident has a contract to support the CIA. Nobody in Trident is an employee or an agent of the CIA."

"Why are you doing the investigation? That sounds like something a CIA agent should do, not a businessman," Diane said.

"I agree with you, but as I said, for some reason the US government isn't too keen on clearing me. Basically, two of the government agencies, the Department of Defense and the Attorney General's office, want to hang me. The CIA is on my side, although the Director of National Intelligence, who the CIA works for, is really pissed off at the scandal Trident has caused," Pat said.

"Let me summarize—you're caught up in a conspiracy inside the US government, and you aren't an agent, but you're going undercover into Iraq and Syria to investigate," said Diane.

"Exactly. What could be easier to understand?" Pat finished his bottle of beer, hoping the conversation was over.

"I've been with you for almost six months and I realize now I don't know anything about you. You told me you were retired from the military, and of course I've seen the scars. But you've never told me a single war story. The scar on your shoulder is the size of a bullet, so I know you weren't a member of the Army band. What did you do in the military?"

With a look of resignation, Pat got up again and retrieved a second bottle of Corona from the mini-bar.

"I was an infantry officer. I started in conventional units and then later in my career moved into some of the more elite special mission units. I was in Afghanistan, Iraq and most of the other hostile places the US has been involved in since the mideighties," said Pat.

"Are you in danger now?"

"No. If I thought I was in danger, I'd make sure you weren't anywhere near me."

"Then why am I going back to the Bahamas?"

"Because you don't have a visa to stay here, for one thing, and for another, I have no idea how long I'll be gone."

"So, I'm supposed to go home to the Bahamas and wait for my soldier to come back to me," Diane said.

"Exactly, and when you get there, you'll find a good-looking Scottish friend of mine staying at the house. His name is Bob McCalister. I can't understand a damn word he says, he's really Scottish, but he'll look after the house and the people in it while I'm away."

"I have a bodyguard?"

"More like bodyguards. Bob is former SAS and MI5. He runs a security company that specializes in that sort of thing. It'll be a lot easier doing what I have to do if I don't have to worry about your safety at home," Pat said.

"You're just full of surprises tonight, aren't you?" Diane asked.

"I'm going to leave the tied-up boat here. When I get back, you can fly back out and we can finish the rest of the trip around the world."

"That sounds like a good idea." Diane slipped into bed and promptly dozed off to sleep.

Pat took the final two swallows of his Corona and stared at the ceiling.

Chapter 7

Sulaymaniyah, Iraq

The C-130 began its rapid descent into the Sulaymaniyah Airport. The irritating noise of the radar lock alarm reverberated in Pat's headset. With the Iranian border less than eighty kilometers to the northeast, the airspace around the airport was heavily contested. Russian, US, French and Iranian air forces all operated in the same general airspace. The Iranian air defenses never interrogated with IFF (identify friend or foe); they just automatically tracked every target within range, indiscriminately causing mayhem by triggering the lock-on defenses of the hapless aircraft.

At two hundred feet above ground level, the plane pulled out of its rapid descent, leveled off and gently touched down midway onto the eight-thousand-foot runway. It taxied to a dilapidated terminal building at the far end of the runway and then pivoted, turning its nose back toward the runway. It was midafternoon, and a blast of heat swept through the cargo hold when the rear cargo ramp dropped. Migos and Sachse released the A7A straps securing the tires of a desert tan Nissan Patrol to the aircraft floor.

After visiting the cockpit and giving his regards to both pilots, Pat returned to the cargo area and hopped into the passenger seat of the Patrol. Sachse shook Pat's hand and wished him well before slamming the heavy armored door shut. Migos started the engine and carefully maneuvered the vehicle down the ramp and onto the tarmac.

"I don't think we're going to find much here. The Peshmerga headquarters we used to deliver to relocated south to Erbil more than a year ago," Migos said.

"Yeah, I know that, but I'm sure they left the records. These guys require three signatures before issuing a bottle of water. That's a ton of paperwork, and it's not something a military force would take with them when advancing on the enemy," Pat said.

"I called a couple of the US military advisors we work with, and nobody had any knowledge of logistics records being left behind," Migos said.

"It's not something that would get a lot of attention. I'm sure whatever happened to the records is below the advisor's radar. We'll start here, and if we don't find what we're looking for, we'll go on to Erbil," Pat said.

Migos wheeled the heavy SUV onto a spot at the edge of the tarmac next to a guarded entrance to the large airport terminal building.

"Those guys in front of the door aren't Peshmerga," Migos said.

All the SUV's windows were darkly tinted, so Pat was unconcerned about alarming the guards as he withdrew a SIG P226 from his shoulder holster, chambered a round and returned it to its holster. Migos did the same, and then both men exited the truck simultaneously.

Seeing the two men, the door guards stood from their shaded chairs and picked up their AKs. Migos greeted the guards in Kurmanji, and Pat could see the men relax as the conversation progressed. After several minutes, the taller guard opened the building door and signaled for Migos and Pat to follow. The two men were ushered into a large room with scattered tables and chairs. Luggage was piled high on one side of the room, while the twelve likely owners of the luggage were lounging and smoking cigarettes on the other side. None of the men wore complete uniforms. Many were wearing scraps of tactical gear and a mishmash of clothing. No two persons had the same body armor, holsters, weapons, tactical vests or combat boots.

The guard led Pat and Migos to two empty chairs and gestured for them to sit.

"What's going on?" asked Pat.

"We're waiting to see the commander. This is the waiting room," said Migos.

"Commander of what?" asked Pat.

"YPG," said Migos.

"Is there any Peshmerga presence still left in the building?" said Pat.

"He wouldn't answer any of my questions. Said we had to talk with the commander," said Migos.

A man dressed in camouflage with a yellow patch on the shoulder with a red star and the letters YPG walked over to the table and sat down. "I heard you guys speaking English. What brings you to Sulaymaniyah?" the man said in perfect English.

"We came here to meet the commander," said Pat.

"Where are you from? You look and sound just like an American," said Migos.

The man smiled. "I'm from Simi Valley California. The name is Marty. What about you?"

"I'm from Boston. My name is Pat and this is Migos."

"What's a guy from California doing in this place wearing a YPG uniform?" said Migos.

The man lit a cigarette. He had long curly black hair and a short beard. The John Lennon glasses and crooked grin combined to give off the impression of a poet rather than a soldier.

The wait to see the YPG commander took over an hour. Migos and Pat killed the time listening to Marty, who never seemed to tire of talking about himself and the cause.

"The YPG has many American fighters. YPG is an acronym that means People's Protective Force. We protect an area in Northern Syria of more than four million people. This airport is our logistics hub. It's where we receive personnel and supplies. These men in the waiting room are all new joiners. Once they're interviewed and approved by the commander, we'll take them to Syria. We aren't an ethnic or a religious faction like most of the groups fighting in this war. Our motives are purely ideological. We're all communists fighting for the Rojava Revolution," said Marty.

"I went to Berkeley and majored in political science," he continued. "After graduation, I spent a full year working on Bernie Sanders's presidential campaign. I was certain Sanders was going to win and we'd finally have social justice in the United States. That was, of course, before the primary election was stolen right out from under him by the Democratic National Committee.

"I had a friend who'd been out here for two years, and he was always asking me to come and join him. Last summer, after the primaries were over and WikiLeaks revealed the extent of the DNC's treachery, I quit the US and took my friend up on his offer. I figured if the corruption in the United States prevents us from building a just government, the next best thing would be to come out here and help to create one myself. It's a revolution and we're the founding fathers," Marty finished.

Another man in a YPG uniform came to Migos and Pat and asked them in English to follow him to the commander's office.

"How much you want to bet the commander is Noam Chomsky?" said Migos as they were walking down the corridor.

"I'm picturing Donald Sutherland in the movie *Kelly's Heroes*," said Pat.

The commander's office was dark, and there were no desk or chairs. It was traditionally decorated, with pillows and cushions against all four walls of the room. When they entered, an elderly man with a white beard wearing ill-fitting fatigues stood and greeted them.

"My name is Colonel Abboud, I'm the commander here," he said in English with a posh British accent.

"It's nice to meet you, sir. Thank you for your hospitality," Pat said.

"I've been conducting newcomer interviews for the past two days, so I welcome the distraction to speak of something else. What brings you two gentlemen to us?"

"Sir, we work for Trident. In 2014, we supplied several shipments to the Peshmerga at this location through the US government. Three years later, the US government is now asking us for delivery receipts. We're undergoing a compliance audit on our export processes. We have all the records the government is requesting except for one receipt voucher, which means we need to obtain the customer copy. The Peshmerga unit we delivered to has since moved, and they didn't take their records. We were hoping we'd be able to find the receipt voucher in the storehouse they left behind at this location," said Pat.

"You came here to find papers to satisfy an audit?" said General Abboud.

"Yes. We realize this is inconvenient for you, and I'm sure you'll want to have personnel overseeing our activities. We will, of course, compensate you for the use of your resources," said Pat.

"You're right—it's a great inconvenience, and I don't have the men to spare," said Colonel Abboud.

"We'll make it worth your while."

"How much did you have in mind?"

"The record storage is big, and the documents are going to be in Arabic and Kurmanji. We'll pay you fifty thousand euros for access to the warehouse and an additional fifty thousand euros if we find the document we're looking for," said Pat.

"You must want that document very badly," said Colonel Abboud.

"If we don't produce it, that could disrupt our business, and that would be very costly," said Pat.

"Seventy-five thousand euros for access, and another seventy-five thousand as a success fee," said Colonel Abboud.

"Agreed." Pat opened his shirt and removed three stacks of fifty five-hundred-euro notes, totaling twenty-five thousand each, from the front pouch pocket of his covert body armor. He dug into his shirt pocket and removed an index card with the English and Kurmanji description and nomenclature of a claymore mine. The list also included the production lot numbers.

"Sir, we're looking for any document with this information on it. Any mention is all we need to prove to the US government that the items were properly delivered," said Pat.

"Tomorrow morning, I'll have a detail of soldiers to help you with your search. In the meantime, if you want to get a head start, I'll have an escort show you into the storehouse," said Colonel Abboud.

The records depot was an abandoned hangar located near the terminal building. With the hangar doors open, the lighting was very good, but the lack of air conditioning was going to make the search uncomfortable.

"Let's just figure out the sorting system, so we can direct the search," said Pat.

"I'll start over there and pull samples from every box," said Migos.

"We're looking at records after May 2014. That's when we delivered the shipment to the Peshmerga," Pat said.

"Boss, you may want to go get the truck and move it into this hangar. The colonel probably thinks you have a stockpile of five-hundred-euro notes in the Nissan," said Migos.

"The truck has bulletproof glass, B-6 armor plating on the sides and roof, and level two blast protection underneath. I doubt any of these communists who have sworn off material wealth could break in," Pat said.

"No kidding. Did you catch the Mao pin on the guy the colonel sent to watch over us?" said Migos.

"For the next few days, or as long as this takes us, it would be best not to make any jokes about Abdullah Ocalan, stateless democracy and democratic confederalism, whatever the heck any of that means," said Pat.

Pat and Migos were leaning on the hood of the Desert Tan Nissan Patrol at the entrance to the hangar serving as the records depot when a gaggle of twenty YPG soldiers arrived. Unlike the group they'd met while in the commander's waiting room, none of the soldiers were American or European—they were all Kurds. Like the soldiers in the waiting room, though, the troops all looked to be clothed and equipped from the military version of a secondhand store.

"Go ahead and brief them and then get them started," said Pat.

Less than an hour into the search, Migos brought a file folder to Pat.

"That was quick. What do we have?"

"This first paper is a requisition list that includes our claymores. The second paper is the delivery receipt. You can see it even includes the same lot numbers," said Migos.

"Does it say who or what unit the items were issued to?" Pat asked.

"It went to an SDF unit called Liwa Ahrar al-Raqqa, which is Arabic for the Free Raqqa Brigade," said Migos.

"Why would the Peshmerga supply them?"

"The Syrian Democratic Forces are a big tent. It includes most of the anti-ISIS and anti-Assad militias. The YPG is part of the SDF. The Free Raqqa Brigade is less well known, but if they promised to help the Peshmerga take Raqqa, it makes sense that they would supply them," Migos said.

"I'll go and pay the money-hungry head communist his seventy-five grand, then we can go find the Free Raqqa Brigade," said Pat.

"Raqqa is at least a twelve-hour drive from here, and getting there will involve a border crossing," said Migos.

"First, I think we need to visit the Peshmerga headquarters running the battle in Mosul. Most of the forces that are going to retake Raqqa are still mopping up the ISIS remnants in Mosul," Pat said.

"I know a lot of the American advisors working with the PUK. We've been ferrying supplies to those guys for a long time," said Migos.

"Who are the PUK again?"

"Patriotic Union of Kurdistan, what you call the Peshmerga."

"Are they the same?" Pat said.

"All PUK are Peshmerga, but not all Peshmerga are PUK."

"Whoever the hell they are, I'm sure they'll help us out. Get the truck ready—I'm going to the colonel's office. Hopefully, he lets me jump the line," said Pat.

"As Karl Marx said, to each according to his needs. That colonel has high needs—no way will he make you wait in line," said Migos.

Pat just shook his head. The knowledge of language, history and culture of the average special forces NCO never ceased to impress him.

When Pat returned from the commander's office, he found the truck with the rear hatch open and Migos working inside.

"Make sure the minigun is loaded and prepped. The commander was very helpful. He told me our unit is operating around Aleppo," Pat said.

"That's going to take at least fifteen hours."

"I think today we'll drive to Erbil and check in with the JSOTF and get an update on the situation. Then tomorrow morning, we can navigate our way to Kobani, where the unit is headquartered," said Pat.

"Between Mosul and Kobani, we're going to have to weave our way through half a dozen different forces. It might be safer at night, when we have the advantage of night vision," Migos said.

"You may have a point. Let's get to Erbil and then decide after we get more information," Pat said.

The drive west to Erbil was mostly on two-lane highways. The roads were clear except when they were going through populated areas. It was sunny and baking hot outside the vehicle, but inside it was dark and cool.

"Where did you get this truck?" said Migos.

"The Presidential Guard is upgrading their VIP protection vehicles. I bought it from them."

"What did you pay for this thing?"

"Four million dirhams, but don't worry—I have a buyer for it if you can keep from wrecking it," said Pat.

"It's a real war wagon, that's for sure. You brought enough ammunition to survive the Alamo."

"Better safe than sorry. Did you figure out how to use the FLIR camera system and the panoramic headset?"

"Not yet," said Migos.

"Pull over. This is really cool, and it works day or night," said Pat. Once the vehicle stopped, Pat removed a pair of virtual reality glasses from a side storage compartment next to the driver. The boxy glasses were Bluetooth-connected, and the screen covered both eyes.

"First thing you do is turn on the external cameras. The vehicle has cameras mounted all around and on top. You can select thermal or day cameras. Let's try thermal," Pat said as he pressed the thermal icon on the main computer console.

"The cameras cover three hundred and sixty degrees, and wherever your head points, the cameras will provide you a seamless picture. You can look in any direction—even up, and you'll have a view of the sky," said Pat.

"This is cool. It's like I can see through the sides of the truck," said Migos.

"Yes. So now, put your hand on the stick shift. The base of the stick shift is a mousepad. Tap it twice and the main menu appears," Pat said. "You can control the remote weapons station with the M134 minigun from your position, or I can do it from my position." Pat put on his own virtual reality glasses.

"To open the roof and elevate the minigun into position, just press deploy on the weapons console. To fire, select arm, and then to engage you have to use the joystick on the armrest. Right hand for you, left hand for me. You can slave the weapon to your headset, so wherever you look, it aims, or you can aim it with the joystick. To redeploy the weapon, just press store."

"This is really badass. What else do we have in the arsenal?" Migos asked.

"Everything else is old-school. We have a McMillan TAC 50 sniper rifle. We have two switchblade exploding UAVs, 2 AT-4s, one DRD Kivaari .338 Lapua in a backpack, and two

Daniel Defense blackout 300 M4s with integrated suppressors. And of course the pistols on our shoulders."

"I'm going to leave my glasses on and practice driving for a while."

"Good idea." Pat reclined his seat.

Migos had flown into the Erbil Airport twice a month for the past year and had little trouble locating the American headquarters. The US had a special forces command post managing the training and advising activities of the Peshmerga, who were mostly behind the action. The battle for Mosul was primarily being waged by the Iraqi Army and not the Peshmerga.

Pat and Migos walked into the building serving as the makeshift headquarters and spoke to a young Special Forces major who was sitting in front a projected display of maps and UAV video feeds. The major was wearing a headset but removed it when the two men approached.

"This is a surprise—the log guys didn't notify me of a supply flight," the major said.

"This is a coordination trip, not a delivery," Migos said. The major diverted his attention to listen to a radio call that was coming over the loudspeaker. He picked up a hand mike.

"Roger, Bravo Seven, stand by. Over," he said. He turned to the Air Force officer sitting at the end of the head table. "What do you have on station?"

"I have two F-16s at the IP and a FAC(A) in the AO," said the officer.

"Get Bravo Seven on the same freq as the FAC(A), he's requesting CAS," said the major as he turned back to Migos and Pat. "What is it you need to coordinate?" he asked them.

"We're looking for the best way to drive to Aleppo. We need to get to a town fifty klicks north, a place called Azas," said Migos.

"Two, give me an INSUM on the drive from here to Aleppo,."

"Yes, sir," said the intelligence captain sitting to the left of the major. The captain changed the display on the wall. The left half was split screen, with the top half showing a UAV feed and the bottom half showing blue icons representing all of the friendly forces. The right half of the screen displayed a map of Iraq and Syria.

"Highway 2 is the fastest route from here to Aleppo, but the safest route is to go north into Turkey, traverse west and then go due south from Gaziantep. Azaz is barely ten kilometers south of the border," said the intel officer.

"That route isn't an option. Turkey won't allow us to cross the border," said Pat.

"Okay, that means you'll have to take Iraq Highway 1 to the Syrian Border and then Syrian Highway M4 to Aleppo. Aleppo has been under bombardment from the Russians, Iranians and Syrians for a hundred and ninety days. When you get to within fifty kilometers of Aleppo, turn off the highway and head due north to Azaz on whatever trail you can find," said the intel captain.

"What's the threat from Mosul to Aleppo and from Aleppo to Azaz?" asked Pat.

"The biggest threat from here to the Syrian border are Shia militias and ISIS. Once you cross the border into Syria, it becomes a mess. There are more than a dozen different factions fighting in and around Raqqa, which you should avoid. From Raqqa to Aleppo and Aleppo to Azaz, you have YPG, Russian, Syrian, Free Syrian, Shia militia, Al-Nusra and Turkish forces, all fighting on the ground. The air situation is equally crowded," said the intel captain.

"What do you recommend for the best time to make the Syrian leg?" said Pat.

"I don't recommend the route at all. A UN convoy was ambushed just yesterday. There are no secure routes," said the intel captain.

"Okay, much appreciated. You guys are busy, we'll get out of your hair."

The two men went back to the truck, where Pat opened a carton of MREs. "Do you want the tortellini or the tacos?"

"I'll take the tacos," said Migos.

Pat and Migos sat in the shade in a couple of camp chairs next to the truck, eating lunch.

"We have all the information you need to prove that it wasn't Trident that diverted the shipment. It's mission accomplished—let's go back to UAE," said Migos.

"We need to find out who diverted the shipment. It's not enough to prove it wasn't us. We need to find out who it was."

"Why? Trident's name is cleared, that should be enough," said Migos.

"Whoever's behind this has to be stopped, and we can't do that unless we know who that is."

"When did stopping terrorists become our job?"

"It's always been our job. That's the reason behind the supplies we ship. Our employer is the CIA. If we can find out who provided those claymores to the Belgium bomber, then the Agency will do the rest," said Pat.

"It might be smarter to call in one of the hercs and fly to Azaz."

"Aleppo International is in a five-way firefight. Assuming we can find an airstrip in or near Aziz to land on, we'd have to fly into airspace contested by the Russians and the Turkish. I think it's safer to drive," Pat said.

"We have a state-of-the-art navigation system, and good off-road capability as long as the sand isn't too soft. Our night vision is like something out of *Star Wars*. I say once we get into

Syria, we stay off the main roads and drive at night," said Migos.

"Agreed. Let's plug a route into the navigation system. Top off the fuel and water and be ready to move in four hours."

Pat was driving and Migos was sleeping. It was 2 a.m. and they had been on the road for ten hours. Pat was wearing the virtual reality goggles and driving at fifty miles per hour parallel to the highway near the city of Raqqa. The truck was fully blacked out, with all the external lights off. He had been able to top off the fuel tanks at a filling station an hour earlier. They were on pace to finish the trip before sunrise.

As Pat crested a hill, he could see the city of Raqqa to the north. Through the thermal cameras, he saw hundreds of hot spots that were fires burning inside the city. At the distance of twenty kilometers, he was too far away to identify any people or vehicles.

Pat slowed the vehicle when he noticed a road block about two kilometers ahead of him, manned by a technical truck. It was a pickup with a heavy machine gun mounted on the cargo bed. The truck was parked at a cut in the road, making it impossible to go around it. Pat and Migos had encountered two road blocks earlier on the trip, but in both cases, they had been able to drive off-road and bypass them. On the first occasion, they had been fired on, but it was only rifle fire, which posed no threat to the truck, which was designed to stop anything up to a 7.62 armor-piercing bullet.

Pat tapped Migos awake.

"What's wrong?"

"There's a roadblock ahead and I can't see any way around it."

Migos put on his headset and conducted his own scan. After conferring with the digital map, he said, "Looks like we'll have to go through them, boss."

"Any idea who they are?"

"My guess would be Assad's forces. This looks like part of the cordon designed to catch civilians and rebels trying to get out of the city," said Migos.

"Once we blow our way through, they're going to know we're here."

"Which do you want, the TAC-50 or the switchblade?"

"Let's take out the truck with the switchblade and the dismounts with the long gun," Pat said.

"I'll take the TAC-50, I've never used the switchblade."

Pat opened the rear door on the SUV and exited the vehicle. Migos withdrew the McMillan TAC-50 hard case. He laid out the sniper's mat at the crest of the hill and started his preparations, extending the bipod and placing the weapon down on the mat. He mounted the Oasys UTCxii Universal Thermal Clip-on in the front and the Schmidt & Bender PM II sniper scope directly behind the UTC.

Migos used the handheld laser range finder to get the range to the road block and then used the Kestrel ballistic computer to get the corrections for windage, elevation and barometric pressure. Pat powered up the ground control station and, with the five-pound tactical missile system under his arm, moved back off the hill so the flash of the launch would not be detectable to the men at the roadblock. He extended the bipod, removed the casing cover and hit the launch button on the ground control station.

Once he spiraled the small UAV up to five hundred feet, he followed the road until he found himself looking down at the thermal signature of a pickup truck. He armed the warhead and dove the munition straight into the Toyota Hilux at a speed of fifty miles per hour.

The Kamikaze UAV detonated at the back of the truck, where the gunner was manning a 12.7mm machine gun. The combination of truck fuel and the munition created a huge blast; the flames and the boom would be seen and heard for miles. As Pat walked back up the hill, he could hear Migos engaging the dismounted personnel still defending the road block. Out of range and unable to even see where Migos's fire was coming from, it took less than twenty seconds before all four dismounts were dead.

Pat jumped in the vehicle and started the engine, while Migos stowed the sniper rifle and then hopped in next to him. The vehicle blew past the still-burning roadblock minutes later.

"Every bad guy in this area is grabbing for his AK right now, so get ready for contact," said Pat.

Migos scanned with his headset while Pat focused on the road.

"Tangos ten o'clock," said Migos.

Looking through thermal cameras made it difficult to see tracers, and the vehicle was pelted by AK fire while they waited the ten seconds for the remote weapons station to lock into place. Once it did, the enemy fire quickly ended when the electric motor kicked in and the six spinning barrels of the M134 Gatling gun generated a fusillade of 7.62 bullets firing at six thousand rounds per minute, obliterating the exposed infantry. Using controlled five-to-ten second bursts, Migos savagely cut down any Syrian crazy enough to expose himself to the gun.

The forty kilometers' drive from Raqqa to Aleppo was disrupted four times by ambushes. The Syrian Army's desperate attempts to stop the SUV were met each time with an overwhelming stream of lead from Migos's mini gun. Twenty kilometers east of Aleppo, Pat turned off the two-lane highway and headed due north to begin the cross-country route to Azaz.

"I'm glad we're off that damn road," said Migos.

"It's almost dawn and we have still have another thirty kilometers to go. We're not out of the woods yet," Pat said.

They were still ten kilometers from Azaz when the sun broke. Pat removed his virtual reality goggles. The added weight to his head was giving him a terrible headache. The stress and adrenaline letdown from the nonstop action over the past few hours only added to his fatigue and discomfort. Pat looked in the mirror. His eyes were bloodshot and the lines on his face attested to the strain. He looked over at Migos and drew comfort seeing that the younger man was holding up a little better.

"Boss, I have a vehicle at ten o'clock, two thousand meters," said Migos.

Pat turned off the trail and into the sandy desert, hoping to bypass it. "Can you identify the vehicle?"

"Negative, but it has turned with us and is moving to intercept us."

"Wheeled or tracked?"

"I think it's tracked and it has a turret," Migos said.

Pat turned ninety degrees to the right. "Are they following?"

"Yeah, looks like they're closing too."

"Must be a tracked vehicle if it can outrun us on this terrain," Pat said.

"What do you want to do?"

"Find a wadi where we can hide, and then we can take him out with the AT-4s."

"There are two vehicles. The lead one is engaging," Migos said. Behind him, Pat could see explosions.

"Twenty-five-millimeter HE," said Pat as he increased speed and sharply turned to the left. The truck was going too fast, bouncing and rocking as it jumped over the uneven terrain.

Another salvo of 25mm rounds exploded fifty meters in front of the SUV, and then Pat finally saw what he was looking for. He yanked the wheel, steered the truck into the wadi entrance and raced the truck down the dry riverbed. He sped through the narrow wadi with high, steep walls that were higher than the SUV until he reached a curve where the wadi widened enough to open the doors.

He slammed on the brakes and skidded to a dusty stop, yanking the rear hatch release, and both men scrambled out of the truck to arm themselves. Pat grabbed the second switchblade, an AT-4 and the Kivaari rifle. Migos picked up his trusty TAC-50 and the second AT-4 84mm rocket-propelled grenade launcher. Pat estimated the vehicles were still fifteen hundred meters away when he launched the switchblade from the hidden recess of the wadi.

"Once I hit the lead vehicle, you pop up with the sniper rifle and take out the track commander on the second vehicle," Pat said as he manipulated the controls of the ground control station, gaining altitude with the UAV. He got the UAV near the target area at only one hundred feet above the ground and armed the bird, and while looking through the thermal camera on the nose of the UAV, he drove it straight into the turret of the advancing lead vehicle.

The track commander who had been standing in the open hatch was blown out of the turret. The vehicle came to sudden burning halt. The back ramp dropped and half a dozen soldiers popped out of the smoking hulk. Migos stood straight on top of the Nissan, placed the bipod of the heavy TAC-50 onto the ledge of the wadi and began engaging the troops as they scrambled for cover. Four of the six dismounts went down to the TAC-50 fire.

Migos was working fast and steady at the bolt action while changing magazines and spotting his own targets. The gunner of the second vehicle located Migos's position and began engaging in five-round bursts. A salvo of 25mm HE exploded on the far side of the wadi, causing Migos to duck.

"The second track is buttoned up and coming fast," Migos said over his comset. Pat slung his rifle over his shoulder and turned to face Migos with the AT-4 in both hands.

"Keep him distracted. I'm going for the flank." Pat raced back to where they had entered the wadi.

Migos was on the hood of the truck in a crouch. He popped up quickly with his TAC-50 and engaged the trail vehicle with three more shots before nimbly ducking down. The second vehicle switched to its coaxial 7.62 machine gun as it continued to close the space while spraying a steady stream of bullets into Migos's last firing position. Migos lay flat on the top of the Nissan as the bullets and tracers snapped over him and sand and rocks sprayed onto him.

As Pat exited the wadi, he found the vehicle less than five hundred meters to his flank and heading straight for Migos. He removed the safety and armed the AT-4 while running unseen toward the vehicle. He was sure the big boxy green M113-like track with the big Bradley-style turret had to be an ACV-15.

When the vehicle got to within two hundred meters of Migos, it stopped and dropped its ramp, disgorging itself of six dismounted infantrymen. The infantry moved forward of the vehicle in formation to clear the wadi under its protective fire.

Pat raced the final fifty meters he needed to make sure he wouldn't miss his target. He slid into a kneeling position, aimed through the pinhole site and depressed the trigger mechanism. The rocket ran straight and true, and the ACV-15 exploded into a huge fireball. The infantry, which had been advancing in a line formation, hit the ground and started firing indiscriminately toward the wadi.

Pat dropped the empty AT-4 tube, unslung his rifle, fell forward into a prone position and began to engage with the Kivaari 338. The infantrymen were less than fifty meters from

Migos's position, their focus directed to their front, where Migos had been engaging them. The infantry began to low-crawl the remaining twenty meters to the wadi.

Migos popped up once more and engaged the advancing soldiers with his 50-caliber sniper rifle. At close range, one soldier bore the full force of the powerful fifty and was flipped from a front crawl onto his back by the enormous force.

Undetected from the flank, Pat picked off the advancing troops with his suppressed .338. At two hundred meters, it was nearly impossible to miss. The soldiers filled the entire view of his eight-power scope. He drilled two of the figures as they attempted to move forward.

The remaining three soldiers, recognizing the situation, attempted to withdraw. The three stood in unison and began to run back to where the first vehicle was still smoking in the distance. Still in the prone, with sand caked to his sweaty face, Pat brought one of the running dismounts into view with his Leupold mil dot scope. As he exhaled, he gently squeezed the trigger and sent a .338 Namo armor-piercing round through the back of the soldier's armored vest.

Migos had his TAC-50 back in full operation on top of the wadi. As Pat was squeezing the trigger on the last escaping dismount, he watched through his scope as the soldier tumbled forward. A second later he heard the discharge from Migos's suppressed weapon. Pat stood, closed the bipod on his rifle and ran back through the wadi entrance and through the ravine until he linked up with Migos at the Nissan.

The two men threw their equipment into the truck and got back into their original seats. Pat drank two one-liter bottles of water and turned the air conditioner on full blast before starting the drive down the wadi.

"Look for a place where we can get out of this wadi," Pat said.

"Roger," said Migos, who had the remote weapons station deployed and focusing behind the truck. After almost two kilometers, the wall of the wadi fell away and the Nissan Patrol was again on the desert floor. Pat turned the vehicle toward Azaz.

"Who were those guys?" said Migos.

"That was the Turkish Army."

"Turkish Army, as in part of NATO Turkey?"

"This place is a fucking free-for-all."

The Nissan was covered in sand and dust as it entered the city of Azaz. At the border of the city were the burned-out remains of a T-72 tank. Most of the buildings within the city had been reduced to rubble, but the roads were mostly clear of debris.

"We need to find a gas station," Pat said.

Still connected to the internet thanks to the vehicles omnidirectional satellite antenna, they were able to find fuel at a place calling itself Faisal Station. After cleaning up and eating an MRE at the gas stop, the two motored into the heart of town, looking for the local YPG Commander. Eventually, they found a building that was mostly intact and had a guard contingent in front.

"Do you remember where I put that claymore paperwork? I'm so tired, I'm starting to forget stuff," said Pat.

Migos withdrew the manila file folders from the door storage area and handed them to Pat. The two got out of the truck and walked to the guards standing in front of the entrance to the building.

"These guys are supposed to have American advisors, it might be better if we ask to see them," said Pat.

Migos launched into his spiel when they reached the guards. Before long the two were following one of the guards into the building and through a narrow labyrinth of corridors until they reached a closed door. The guard knocked on the door and a bearded American wearing a wife beater t-shirt and ACU pants opened the door.

"My name is Migos, this is Pat Walsh, it's good to see you," said Migos. The American was clearly surprised by the visit, but he recovered quickly.

"Come on in, my name is Taylor, this other guy is Dillon, but he likes to be called pecker head," said Taylor. Dillon had a bald head and bushy red beard, he looked like he would make a good rampaging Viking.

Dillon and Taylor were excellent hosts. They brought Migos and Pat coffee and allowed them to shower, shave and get a change of clothes. Migos told the story of the adventurous drive from Erbil to Aziz. He left out the part about the engagement with the Turks, thinking that would probably create an international incident. Both men were with the 3rd Special Forces Group. Migos told him he was formerly 5th Group and he mentioned that Pat was a Ranger and former CAG to help establish Trust.

"What is it you men want?" said Dillon.

"We're contractors working for DOD. Back in April there was suicide bombing in Belgium, it killed almost two hundred people. The explosives used were claymores that we delivered to the Peshmerga in Erbil. The Peshmerga issued part of the stock to your unit, now we're trying to find out where it went from there," said Pat.

"We do get logistics support from Erbil, that much sounds right. How do you know we received the claymores in question?" said Dillon?

"We have the hand receipt that has a long laundry list of items issued included the claymores," said Pat.

"Mind if I see it?" said Dillon. Migos gave Dillon the folder.

"Why don't you guys get some sleep. We have some empty bunks down the hall. The unit has a logistics office and everything that comes in and goes go out gets recorded and signed for. I'll let you know once I find something," said Dillon.

The two exhausted men slept until the next morning.

"Migos, you look like your old self," said Pat.

"I feel a lot better. Six tours in Iraq and that drive was the hairiest damn thing I have ever done," said Migos.

"That which doesn't kill you will only make you stronger," said Pat.

"Conan the barbarian quotes aren't exactly my idea of inspiration," said Migos.

"The area around Aleppo is positively medieval. The Russians and Syrians are bombarding the city and ISIS is shooting kids to force families to remain in the city and serve as human shields. Conan would be right at home in this place," said Pat.

Pat and Migos were at the vehicle, cleaning and oiling the weapons when Dillon came to them.

"I got the answer to your question," he said. Dillon handed over the file folder he received from Migos the day before and opened it.

"This is the issuing paperwork to one of our YPG units that was operating out of Azaz. They didn't record the lot numbers, but you can see the numbers match the total issued to the Command. It's safe to say they received the full load," said Dillon.

"Can we talk to the Commander of the unit to find out what he did with them?" said Pat.

"The Commanders name was Major Meer Abbas. He was killed when most of his unit was wiped out back in February," said Dillon.

"Can you give me the details?" said Pat.

"I remember the incident well, I wrote enough reports about it. On February 17 of this year, Major Abbsas and

Kandak Twenty-One were operating in the vicinity of Marea, a town only ten kilometers south of here toward Aleppo. The unit had seventy-eight fighters and was in a defensive position when they were overrun by a local militia called Fursan al-Haq, which means Knights of Righteousness."

"What happened?" Pat asked.

"Fursan al-Haq is another SDF unit. They're supposed to be playing for the same team as the YPG. They took our guys by surprise in a night raid. I was in the operations center trying to get air support approved. We had two American-backed units fighting each other, and the guys in the head shed wouldn't support one side against the other, so they stood down and allowed our guys to get completely destroyed," Dillon said.

"These units were on the same side," Migos said with a disbelieving tone.

"The militias are managed by the CIA. The YPG is managed by Department of Defense. The militias have diverse agendas. They're much harder to control. This particular group doesn't want the Kurdish influence to extend into Aleppo. When the civil war is over, they don't want to have lost any land to the Kurds. Destroying the YPG element closest to Aleppo was their way of communicating a limit of advance to the YPG," Dillon said.

"Where can we find the Knights of Righteousness?" Pat said.

"They still operate out of Marea. The commander is a guy named Major Yasser Abd al-Rahim. The fucker did interviews with the news media after he slaughtered our people. If you're paying him a visit, feel free to put a 9mm through his face."

"How do we know they captured the claymores?" Migos said.

"We can't be sure until we talk with them," Pat said.

"I knew you were going to say that, I fucking knew it," Migos said.

"Thanks for your help, Dillon. Let's get this war pig up and get ready to roll," Pat said.

Pat used his phone camera and took photos of all the paperwork. Then he typed up an email summarizing the investigation and sent it encrypted over the tactical satellite to Mike Guthrie at CIA Headquarters in Langley. It was noon, and the two were sitting in the air-conditioned truck still parked in front of the YPG headquarters in Aziz.

"Maybe we should contact the Agency and ask for help on this next part. The Knights of Righteousness work for the same people we do," said Migos.

"I'm guessing they're hard to control. If they didn't have a CIA advisor before they attacked the YPG in February, I'm sure they do by now."

"We just need to get in touch with that guy. Can you call your buddy? Maybe he can get you the local agent's cell number and we can do a linkup, or better yet, get what we need by phone."

"Probably not a good idea. If those claymores fell under the control of the Knights of Righteousness, they wouldn't willingly give them to ISIS. Those guys are fighting ISIS around the outskirts of Aleppo. Nobody is going to arm their enemy."

"Which means they probably lost them to ISIS in a battle."

"That's one explanation. The other is far more menacing. The ISIS units in Aleppo aren't attacking and seizing supplies, they're escaping. The SDF units are cordoning Aleppo and shooting the ISIS fighters as they try to flee while at the same time helping the local population get out of the city," Pat said.

"I get your point. Seems pretty unlikely any ISIS fighters captured the claymores from the Knights of Righteousness."

"Yeah, we're going to have to be careful when we talk to that commander."

It was two in the afternoon when they rolled into Marea. The thermometer display on the truck dashboard showed the outside temperature at One hundred and fourteen degrees. The town was barely a square kilometer in size and consisted of a couple of dozen small one-story concrete buildings and a handful of taller four- to five-story structures.

Twenty kilometers beyond Marea was Aleppo, which could barely be seen through the pall of smoke and dust that hung over that portion of the desert. With only two main roads in the town, it was easy to find the Knights of Righteousness command post. It was stifling hot and the unit had no guards posted, just a unit banner hanging inside a broken front window.

Migos parked the truck and the two men exited the vehicle wearing full tactical gear, complete with helmets and body armor. Both men wore subdued American flags attached to the Velcro of their multicam UF PRO uniforms. Once they were inside the doorway, a guard at the reception station stood up and attempted to bring his AK-47 to a ready position.

"Take a seat and relax. We're here to meet the commander," Migos told the guard in Arabic.

The two rifles pointed at his head were all the convincing the guard needed as he quickly sat down. The building had no power, which eliminated the second floor as an office location for the commander. Pat and Migos walked past the reception desk and down the only corridor, looking for the man in charge. At the last office, they found a second receptionist. The receptionist stood to block Pat, who was in the lead, but Pat pushed the man aside, opened the door and walked into the commander's office, holding his blackout 300 ISR rifle in a ready position.

Inside the office, Pat could see a fat middle-aged man with a beard and mustache sitting behind a large steel desk, who Pat took to be the commander. Sitting on a chair in front of the desk was a much fitter and better groomed middle-aged Arabic man. There were two other Arab men sitting in chairs along the wall.

"Are you Major al-Rahim?" said Migos in Arabic.

"Yes, who are you?" said the major in English.

"We work for the United States government. We'd like to ask you a few questions in private," Migos said. The man seated in front of the desk stood up. He was five foot ten and thin, with steel-grey eyes, a short salt-and-pepper beard and a sneering facial expression.

"My name is Fouad Zhattari. I'm the only person authorized to represent the US government in Marea," he said in English.

"I'm going to have a private discussion with the commander, Fouad. You don't want to challenge me on this," said Pat, raising his rifle to Fouad's chest.

"I'll meet with these two men alone. Please go," Major al-Rahim said to Fouad and the two subordinate officers in the room. After the three men departed, Pat and Migos sat across from the commander, who remained seated behind his desk.

"In April, one hundred and seventy-five Belgians were killed by an ISIS suicide bomber in Brussels. The attacker detonated six claymore mines in a crowded square. The lot numbers on those mines were identified in the residue of the blast, and the last known whereabouts of those claymore mines was here in Marea, under your control. Migos, show him the paperwork," said Pat. Migos showed the major the documents and explained in a mixture of Arabic and English how the explosives had been traced from Erbil to Azaz to Marea.

"Now we know you hate Daesh and would never supply your enemy. But we need to know what happened to those claymores after they came under your ownership," said Pat.

"What if I refuse to help?" said the major.

"Then I'll kill you and everyone else in this building and conduct a records search until I find what I'm looking for," said Pat.

"You realize that man you just threw out of my office works for your government? He's with the CIA," said the major.

"He's my primary suspect. I'll shoot him second, right after you I kill you," said Pat.

The major sat looking at the paperwork. For a warrior, he looked very much at home behind the desk. After a few seconds of consideration, he stood up.

"Come with me. My logistics office is down the hallway. We'll see what we can find," said the major.

"Only you and the logistics officer have a need to know. Don't tell anyone else what we're after," said Pat.

"We're partners in this fight, Americans and my people. There's no need for force," said the major.

"Tell that to the YPG in Aziz," Pat said.

As they walked down the corridor, they passed Fouad's office. He was standing next to the window talking on a satphone, clearly angry. The logistics office was small, the furniture consisting of only a few file cabinets and a small desk. The logistics officer had the appearance of an academic. He was roughly sixty years old, grey and thin. Pat was unable to understand the rapid conversation between the major and the logistics officer. On two occasions, the logistics officer opened the file cabinet and withdrew paperwork. After twenty minutes of heated conversation, the he made a call on his cell phone.

"What's going on?" Pat asked Migos.

"He has a record of having forty claymores in his stock. He doesn't have a record of issuing any. He said the units aren't trained to use them and have no need of them," said Migos.

"Where are those mines now?" Pat asked.

"He just called the arms depot and asked them to count the inventory."

"We should head there ourselves, although I think I already know the answer."

When they passed Fouad's office again, Pat noticed that it was empty. The unit wisely stored ammunition outside of the blast range of the headquarters, and so they had to walk five hundred meters in the heat down the main road, past several badly damaged buildings until they came across one that was mostly intact. The arms depot was a single-story building with only three rooms. They kept ammunition in one room, weapons in another, and the third room served as a dorm for a three-man guard force.

Pat and Migos were escorted to a stack of three wooden boxes marked M68 Claymore Mines. The cases were wrapped in metal bands, and the latch securing each box was wired and sealed.

"None of these boxes has ever been opened," said Migos.

"One of the boxes is missing. They're marked ten per—where's the fourth box?" said Pat. Migos translated Pat's question to the head guard/supply clerk, but all he got in return was a shrug.

"Can you find out who has access to this room?" said Pat.

After ten minutes of back-and-forth with the commander and the head guard, Migos addressed Pat. "Only the commander, the three guards and two other officers have access," he said.

"What about the CIA?" said Pat.

"Only escorted, same as us," said Migos.

"It could be that the fourth box was never recovered from the YPG and never made its way here," said Pat.

"That could be it," said Migos.

"They should have a log of everyone who's come into this place, what gets delivered and what gets issued. Normally with these guys, the commander has to sign everything, because with these militias, all this stuff is his personal property. Where's that log?" Pat asked.

The guard quickly retrieved a large green book and brought it to the commander. The commander did not share the book with Migos. Instead, he spent a good ten minutes reading it, starting at a point midway in the book. Finally, the commander lifted his head up.

"Four cases of claymores were delivered to this room. There are no records of any claymores being issued," he said.

"I'm going to need to take a picture of the entry where it shows four cases being present," Pat said.

The page was opened and presented to Pat, who snapped a photo of the page with his iPhone.

"You have what you came for. You're no longer welcome in Marea. It's time for you to go," he said before turning to his officers and speaking to them in a hostile animated tone. The commander was clearly furious at his staff.

The long walk back to the truck gave Pat and Migos time to plan. "You wanna go talk to that CIA agent?" said Migos.

"I don't see the point. I think we've already overstayed our welcome. Let's give the truck a complete once-over before we leave."

"We're looking for tracking devices?" said Migos.

"Tracking devices and things that go boom."

"Maybe going in strong wasn't the best idea."

"I think if we'd gone in soft, we'd still be waiting to see the commander. Force is the only thing these people understand," Pat said.

"I wonder where Fouad went to," Migos said.

"He's going to have a lot to explain. I imagine right now he's making sure his version of how a crate of claymores got lost from his arms room and blew up hundreds of people in downtown Brussels gets to the higher-ups before our version of events," Pat said.

"Do we even have a version of events?"

"Not yet, we just have a few key facts. How the claymores got to Belgium is still a mystery, but we're getting closer to figuring that out every day."

"How about I drive and you man the remote weapons station?"

"Sound good," Pat said as he dropped flat and crawled under the Nissan with a small Maglite in his hand.

The ten-kilometer drive back to Aziz took them along the same twisted dirt trail they'd used on the way out. The terrain was rocky and hilly, dotted by the occasional semi-demolished building. Pat kept the minigun deployed on top of the vehicle in the firing position and used the virtual reality glasses to methodically scan the forward landscape with the magnified day cameras. Migos concentrated on navigating the narrow, twisting trail at the fastest speed possible.

The Nissan was cresting a hill when the passenger side of the front end erupted in an enormous explosion that lifted the front of the truck off the ground and rocked all four tons of the heavily armored SUV. Dazed by the explosion, Pat sat unmoving in the passenger seat of the truck as he watched the windshield spiderweb from rifle and machine gun fire. As his hearing returned, the sounds of bullets cracking off the bulletproof glass filled the air. The volume of fire intensified until the noise of bullet impacts began to sound like popcorn popping.

Regaining his senses, Pat grabbed the controls and lit up the surrounding hills with the minigun, spraying twenty-second bursts across the full-frontal arc of the vehicle. The firing dissipated and Pat began engaging the targets with more precision so as not to melt the machine gun. He caught a man with an RPG-7 as he was raising it to his shoulder.

"Three hundred meters, two o'clock," Migos shouted.

"On the way," Pat said as he hosed a squad of ambushers down with a thousand rounds of 7.62mm ball in four even bursts. A mortar round exploded a hundred meters in front of the vehicle.

"Grab a bag and a weapon and get ready to bolt," Pat ordered, turning around and pulling the medium-sized backpack located directly behind his passenger seat onto his lap. "On the count of three, open your door and bail. I'll cover you, and then I'll follow you out the same door. We'll link up behind that hill."

Migos opened the heavy armored door and rolled out of the vehicle. Pat covered Migos's exit with the minigun. He fired the remaining rounds from the huge magazine in two long bursts. Reaching back into the cargo compartment, he pulled the heavy TAC-50 case onto his lap, then crawled across the seat and exited the open driver's door. He used the vehicle for cover as he slid on a backpack, slung his carbine on and cradled the heavy TAC-50 case. Another mortar round exploded fifty meters behind the truck, which prompted a heavily burdened Pat to scramble behind the same hill where Migos was waiting.

Sprinting seventy-five meters uphill wearing body armor and a heavy backpack while carrying the TAC-50 caused Pat's legs and chest to burn with exertion. The rifle and machine gun fire from the ambush position had stopped. The mortar forward observer must have finished bracketing the truck, because just then, a salvo of twelve 82mm mortar rounds exploded all around the truck, completely destroying it.

"We need to get out of here before that forward observer targets us," said Pat.

"Where's the FO?" said Migos.

"On the other side of the trail somewhere. Let's stay behind this cover and try to find a spot on the other side of the hill to spot him," said Pat. The two men scrambled down the slope and moved due north along a shallow valley. A mortar round exploded one hundred meters behind them. They traversed several hundred meters around the hill until they once again had a vantage point of the trail, Pat dropped the TAC-50.

"Get this ready, I'm going to spot for that observer," said Pat. Using the six-power magnified sight on his rifle, he started from the left and slowly unmasked himself from behind the hill. He drew a line on the sand with a T at the end and ducked back behind the sandy hill.

"When I say go, put the weapon on the line with the bipod on the T. There are two targets located sixteen hundred meters out, along that line. Go to the top of the hill and you'll find them about twenty-meters below the crest," said Pat.

"Are you ready?" said Pat. Migos had the rifle fully assembled and in the carry position, and he made small adjustments to the range and windage knobs on the scope.

"Ready," Migos said.

"Go."

Migos quickly stepped forward and slid into a prone position with the bipod at the T and the weapon on the line. Pat got behind Migos in a kneeling position with his weapon trained on the target.

"I'll spot, do you have them?" Pat said.

"Affirmative."

The first shot decapitated a man holding a pair of binoculars. Seeing the first man drop, the second began to scramble up the hill to escape. A 50-caliber sniper round hit him in the back just as he reached the top of the hill. The force of the impact drove him forward and out of sight.

Migos sat up behind the TAC-50 and took a long drink of water from the hydration pack built into the go-bag Pat had just dropped to his side. "Now who the fuck are those guys?"

"Move this gun to where you can cover me. I'm going to grab one of them and find out."

"We need to get out of here," Migos said.

"The ambush line is less than a klick from here. Someone will be wounded we can talk to."

"We should both go. They won't be English speakers."

"I hate to lose the sniper cover," Pat said.

"With this .338 and this scope, I can easily hit a man at fifteen hundred meters," Migos said, pointing to the Kivaari.

"Okay, it's bounding over watch. You cover, I'll move," said Pat.

By the time they reached the hill where they had been ambushed from, the sun was setting. The first four men they found were dead. None of the men wore body armor, and they had all been hit dozens of times by the minigun.

"I found one," Migos yelled.

"Can he speak?" Pat asked as he reached Migos's position next to the badly wounded man.

"Yeah. He says he's with Suquor Al-Jabal. He and sixteen other men set the ambush. It was short notice. He's low-level. He doesn't know anything else," said Migos.

"Does his unit have Amerikis?"

Migos prodded the barely conscious man. "Yes, they have American advisors," he said.

"CIA or military?"

After more exchanges in Arabic, Migos replied, "He doesn't know."

"Find out the name of the American advisor."

Migos could no longer get the man to respond to his questions. "I think he's gone."

"Let's go back to Azaz."

It was dark, and the two men walked in the desert, paralleling the trail. The desert was quiet, a full moon had risen, and the visibility was good enough to make night vision goggles unnecessary. There was a gentle wind, and although the temperature was eighty-two degrees, it felt cool. The men left the heavy TAC-50, taking the bolt and the sight to make it inoperable. They carried only the rifles and backpacks.

On their arrival to Azas, Migos and Pat went into the Knights of Righteousness Headquarters and located Dillon.

"What happened to you guys?" Dillon asked as he took in the sight of the two filthy and exhausted men.

"We got ambushed coming out of Marea, by a group calling themselves Suquor Al-Jabal. Any idea who they are?" said Pat.

"They're another Sunni militia group. They're anti-Kurd and anti-ISIS, same as the guys in Marea."

"Do they work closely with the Knights of Righteousness?" said Pat.

"I don't know. We don't have much communications with the CIA-led units. We try to stay clear of them, and they try to stay clear of us."

"This whole thing is just as fucked up as Hogan's goat," Migos said. He dropped his backpack and leaned the rifle on it. "I mean, we got American units fighting American units. We got Turkish forces fighting American units. We got ISIS fighting American units. We got Russians fighting American units, and we got Syrians fighting American units. Oh, and let's not forget the Iranians. How do you stand this, Dillon?"

"The Kurds are good people. You're right about everything else. Once ISIS is dealt with, this is going to turn into one big cluster," Dillon said.

"Do you mind if we crash in the same room as before? We'll be gone tomorrow morning," Pat said.

"No problem."

The two men closed the door to their room. It had a lone overhead light and two beds with thin, dirty mattresses.

"How are we going to get out of here tomorrow morning?" Migos said.

"By truck, we're going to drive through the Turkish Border and then partake in first-class accommodations back to UAE," Pat said.

"I like the idea, but how are we going to get a truck?"

"We're going to buy one with the money you brought." Pat pointed to Migos's backpack.

Migos opened his pack for the first time and dumped the contents onto the bed. Ammunition, strobe lights, MREs, water, hygiene kit, poncho liner and energy bars fell out along with two brick-sized cellophane-wrapped packages.

"No wonder that bag was so heavy. How much is this?" Migos said.

"That's half a million bucks. And it weighs less than twelve pounds, so stop complaining," Pat said as he undressed and headed for the shower.

Chapter 8

Istanbul, Turkey

Pat and Mike Guthrie sat side by side in a pair of wicker chairs on the terrace of the hotel suite. The Ritz-Carlton was a grand aging hotel with some of the best views in Istanbul. Perched high on the European side above Vodaphone Park and Taksim Square, the hotel overlooked the dark waters of the Bosporus. Beyond the narrow strait connecting the Baltic to the Sea of Marmara was the Asian landmass.

On the small table between the two chairs sat a half-empty bottle of Glen Grant 18 and two tumblers. The two men had been slowly drinking for almost two hours with scarcely a word spoken.

The noise from the street traffic six floors below was distant enough to be barely noticeable except for the occasion car horn. It had been a hot, muggy summer day, and as the cooler evening set in, the tourists began to emerge along the steep city streets.

"Why did you choose Istanbul?" Mike said.

"I wasn't sure if the next move was going to be a return to Aleppo or moving on to Belgium," Pat said.

"What info are you looking for to decide?"

"I need you to come clean with me, Mike. The trail ended in Matea, and the last signpost read CIA."

"You think our people are involved?"

"Yes. I can't prove it, but I think so," Pat said.

"Why?"

"The chain of custody of the claymores used in Brussels ends in Marea, Syria, under the control of the Knights of Righteousness. The physical evidence is strong. The advisors for the Knights of Righteousness are your people. After Migos and I uncovered the loss of the claymores, we were ambushed on our way back to Aziz. The unit that ambushed us was Suquor Al-Jabal, yet another CIA-supported Shia militia group. There's no way either one of those Shia militias went into that arms room, stole the mines and gave them to their most-hated enemies, which are the Sunni ISIS."

"You think Fouad Zhattari took the claymores and gave them to ISIS?" Mike asked.

"He made a point of disappearing. I think he knew of or was involved in taking the claymores, and I think he gave them to ISIS, or to someone else who gave them to ISIS. I also think he tried to have Migos and myself killed."

"You better be careful who you talk to about this. You don't have a lot of facts to back up that kind of an accusation," said Mike.

"No, I don't, and out of respect for you, I'm not going after Fouad to force him to give up the truth. I think that's something the Agency should handle themselves."

"Given your history, I appreciate what you mean by that. How is your man Migos?" said Mike, changing the subject.

"He's fine. He left the sandbox unbloodied and a thick bundle of Benjamins richer. That guy is a prize."

"Maybe I should hire him," Mike said with a grin.

"Give it your best shot. He's developing expensive tastes, I doubt you can afford him."

Pat walked across the terrace and turned on some music on the hotel's Bose speaker system. Using his iPhone, he selected the *Guardians of the Galaxy I* soundtrack. "Did you see this movie?"

"No, what is it?"

"*Guardians of the Galaxy.* I have a second bedroom in this place. We'll watch it tonight. It's hilarious, and it's about saving the universe, kind of like your job," Pat said.

"I have to run in a few minutes. The next step isn't Belgium, and it isn't Syria. You should hold tight. I need to go back and consult with the senior management. We need to look into our operations and our people in Marea, and that's going to be a sensitive subject that may take some time," Mike said.

"If it's going to be a few weeks, I'll go back to Abu Dhabi and continue on with my plan to sail and surf around the world," Pat said.

"This is going to take at least that long. Where are you going next?"

"Phuket and Bali are on the list, but I need to add a few other stops because of fuel."

"That's a good idea. It'll keep you out of trouble. I'll call you when I have something."

After Mike let himself out, Pat poured himself some more scotch. He took a sip and searched his senses in an attempt to detect the rich pastry-like sweetness, honey and soft apricots the whiskey review mentioned. The track playing was Elvin Bishop's "Fooled Around and Fell in Love."

The debate swirling around his mildly intoxicated head was whether or not to bring Diane along when he continued the sailing cruise. The key issue centered around risk. He wasn't sure of the risk, because he couldn't figure out who was after him and why. None of the facts added up. He refilled his glass as he pondered what he knew.

The ambush in Syria could only have been triggered by the CIA. All CIA Middle East clandestine operations fell under Mike. Pat had always been able to trust Mike, and he saw no reason for that to change now. How could someone working under Mike be involved with attacking two CIA assets who were investigating under Mike's direction? Mike and the CIA director had personally intervened with the president to remove the sanctions against his business. It seemed impossible the CIA would now be working against him. Pat was convinced Mike was on his side and that Mike would get to the bottom of whatever was going on within his own organization. Fouad Zhattari was no doubt already being recalled to Langley for questioning.

The case against Fouad would not be hard to press. There were a lot of questions that needed answers. Did Fouad have prior knowledge of his unit's assault against the YPG? Fouad seemed pretty buddy-buddy with the Knights of Righteousness commander; it was hard to believe he hadn't known of the attack plan. And if he knew about the plan to attack the YPG, why hadn't he stopped it? Once the attack was over, had Fouad reported the captured YPG munitions and equipment through his agency chain of command? Had the claymores been supplied to ISIS because someone had known they were supplied by Trident?

But why would anyone care enough about Trident to conduct such an atrocity? Even if they put Trident out of business, another contractor would eventually take over the contract. Trident was far from irreplaceable. What was Fouad's knowledge of the claymores, of Trident and of the attack on the YPG?

Those were all questions Pat wanted to ask, but he knew he would never be given the chance. The more he thought about the situation, the more he was able to talk himself out of the idea that questioning Fouad would finish the investigation. Whatever was going on was still unclear to him. Getting answers from Fouad would definitely provide the breadcrumbs to the next stop, but it was not going to explain the connection between Trident and Brussels, he was sure of that.

With so much uncertainty, Pat decided not to bring Diane out but to continue the sailing trip alone. He felt much more comfortable with her at home with Bob and his team.

Chapter 9

Camp de Pêche de la Rivière Moisie, Quebec

Michael Genovese approached the fishing camp in the backseat of an Augusta Westland AW109 Grand. The trip from Manhattan to Quebec had taken a little over two hours. The interior of the luxury helicopter was surprisingly quiet and smooth. The helicopter was flying at two hundred and forty knots at three hundred feet above ground level over the deep blue expanse of the St. Lawrence River, which separated New Brunswick from Quebec. Once across the St. Lawrence, they passed into the Canadian province of Quebec.

Michael felt the helicopter drop speed and descend while banking right to fly upstream along the Moisie River. The shallow water of the Moisie appeared brown from his vantage, and both side windows were filled with steep banks and rocky cliffs. Beyond the banks was a virgin coniferous forest devoid of any roads or trails.

After less than five minutes tracing the winding Moisie River, they approached a river island with a camp consisting of a large log house and ten smaller cabins arrayed along the outer perimeter. The aircraft touched down on a lush green lawn in the center of the island.

Michael collected his heavy field bag and his Orvis Fly Rod Case and headed directly to cabin number four. This was not his first trip to the fishing camp, and he knew exactly where to go. The cabin was rustically designed while still managing to offer all the modern amenities, including internet and television.

Michael rushed to unpack his fishing equipment. He threw on a pair of Orvis hip waders, an L.L. Bean vest, and his lucky Smith Optical glasses, and grabbed his rod and the small case containing his favorite flies before heading out to the river at a trot.

The Moisie River was one of the most significant spawning grounds for the North Atlantic salmon in North America. The season had officially ended more than a month earlier, but the revenue the camp brought to the local economy bought leniency in such matters. Michael could hear the gentle babble of the river as he approached the shallow bank.

Two men were standing knee-deep in the flowing river, both anglers casting into the same pool. The two men were in rhythm as they cast and retrieved their flies, skillfully avoiding snagging the other's line on the surface of the still, dark water. Michael waved to the two men, who acknowledged him with a head nod.

With the best spot taken, Michael moved downstream fifty meters and set up. He slipped his net into a pocket in the back of his vest. From a breast pocket of his vest, he withdrew a small patch of wool that held three of the best flies. Without hesitation, he chose the black bear red butt. With practiced precision, he tied the fly to the tippet on his leader. Wasting no time, Michael stepped into the current. He almost lost his balance, but soon found his footing on the round stones. The cool water was midway up his thigh as he eased his body slightly into the current and made his first cast upstream.

After four hours of tireless fishing, Michael watched a salmon hit his fly from below and jump into the air. His reel began to whir as the line played out. He was careful not to allow too much tension on the fragile four-pound line and the delicate eight-foot rod. Michael played the fish with patience and skill, releasing the line when the fish ran and drawing it in when the fish rested. He allowed the salmon to fully exhaust itself before gradually reeling the fish in to his position and collecting it from the water with his net. At thirty inches and twelve pounds, it was an excellent catch. Michael was sure it was the biggest catch of the day as he sloshed toward the bank, holding the fish above his head by the gill. The triumphant expression on Michael's face was reflective of the picture in his mind, which was that of General McArthur in the famous newsreels of him wading to shore on his return to Manila in World War II.

The six campers convened for dinner in the main fishing lodge building. The lodge had three rooms plus a screened-in back porch that sat on pylons overhanging the river. The décor held to the rustic theme found in the rest of the camp and consisted of log walls, rough-hewn wooden furniture, lantern-shaped lights and stone fireplaces in each room. The dining room was dominated by a huge distressed heavy wooden table that could seat twenty-two people. The second room was a library with brown leather recliners and dozens of oak shelves filled with hardcover classics. The third was a billiard room, which, in addition to a professional-grade pool table, had a long, well-stocked bar complete with a gleaming mahogany countertop, brass rail and leather stools.

Camp de Pêche de la Rivière Moisie was an elite club visited by some of the richest men in America, established in the early nineteenth century. The first owners were Boston bluebloods. Adams, Cabot and Winthrop were the family names of the founders. At the time of the camp's creation, they were among the most affluent men in the region. The property had been perpetually held in family trusts and rarely ever sold or transferred. Despite the Brahmans' twin aversions to large families and ostentatious consumption, it was inevitable that over time, the value of the individual trusts would dwindle. At one hundred and fifty thousand dollars per week, few of the owners' descendents could afford to stay at their ancestral holiday spot, and it was instead used by scions of industry for corporate retreats and other such gatherings.

After turning his catch over to the camp cooking staff, Michael returned to his cabin to shower and prepare for dinner. When he entered the main lodge building, Michael noticed he was the last to arrive. Five men were seated at the dining table. The highlight of the meal was his grilled wild salmon. Although several of the other campers had had success and hooked a salmon during the afternoon, they'd all engaged in "catch and release," a concept whose logic completely evaded him.

The men were in high spirits. The wine was flowing and the conversation was lively. The men surrounding the table all headed Fortune 500 companies. They were business associates and friends, and they were all men of significance in the defense industry.

After dinner, the men retired to the screened-in porch area. A cool breeze passed through the open porch, causing most of the men to cover up with fleece or a windbreaker. The men sat in Adirondack chairs in a circle surrounding a wrought-iron gas-fueled fire pit that provided a campfire ambience and some warmth. Michael held a bottle of Alexander Keith India Pale Ale in his hand and appraised the group. To Michael's right sat Mitch Vogel, the chairman and CEO of Ball, Inc. Ball was a Texas-based aerospace company that manufactured several of the helicopters used by the USMC, including the latest VTOL. Vogel was seventy-six years old. He had been a UH-1 "Huey" pilot in the sixties and had served three tours in Vietnam. He'd joined Ball as soon as he'd left the service and for the next forty-five years worked his way up from a production supervisor job to one day owning a controlling interest in the company.

Next to Mitch Vogel sat Jonathan Garthwaite. JG Technologies was the leader in IED countermeasures. Virtually every NATO vehicle sported a JG Technologies jamming system. Garthwaite had been a professor of electrical engineering at Carnegie Mellon in the midnineties, when DARPA had begun funding research into jamming technologies to defeat remote-control explosives. Garthwaite had formed JG Technologies in 2001, just a couple of years before the market for such systems had literally and figuratively boomed.

Next to Garthwaite sat Jason Truesdale, the sixty-two-year-old CEO of Arizona-based HTK Corp. HTK was the largest ammunition, medium gun and turret manufacturer in the United States. Making everything from small-caliber rifle bullets to heavy artillery shells, HTK had seventeen subsidiaries. In 1996, when Truesdale had been an executive at Blackstone Private Equity, he had orchestrated a leveraged buyout and deposed the founder of HDK. His reward for the hostile takeover, beyond the industry tradition of a crystal tombstone, had been the CEO position, a job he had held ever since.

To the right of Truesdale sat Matthew Patterson. Patterson was the seventy-eight-year-old founder of Oswagee Defense, which had originally been Oswagee Trucks. In 2003, the US military had tendered a rush requirement for mine-resistant ambush-protected (MRAP) vehicles, and Patterson had decided to experiment with armoring the cabs of his tractor-trailers.

Seated to Patterson's right and Michael's left, completing the circle, was David Cohen. Cohen was the chairman and CEO of Cohen Communications, the industry-leading manufacturer of RF Radio Systems. Cohen's father had been a NASA engineer who had founded the company in Florida in the 1970s. Cohen and Michael were the only two members at the gathering younger than forty. Both had attended Harvard together, although Cohen was three years senior to Michael.

The men continued the jovial banter from the dinner table for several minutes, until there was an awkward pause and Michael noticed the other men were all looking toward Mitch Vogel.

"Michael, I have been asked to speak for the group," he drawled in his west Texas twang. "This business in Brussels was not okay with us. All of us in this circle are loyal Americans. We're patriots. We have done some things that may have bent the law at time, but they were always justifiable for the greater good. Blowing up innocent people in Europe crosses a line none of us ever intended to cross. You need to understand, it isn't something we would have ever given our consent to. This isn't what we signed up for when we organized this group," Vogel said.

"It was the only option. It had to be done. We risked exposure, and it was the best way to remove a threat that could have put every man in this room in prison," said Michael.

"Before you take actions like that, you need to consult with the group. What you did was done without our approval," Vogel said.

"All of you benefit from what I do, but none of you ever get your hands dirty. I'm surprised you even know the details of my involvement in Brussels. Either way, it was my action to take, and I took it. It can't be turned back," said Michael in a calm, controlled voice.

"Hold on for just a minute. No need to get defensive. How about you explain the what and the why on this, and maybe we can all agree with you that it was a good move?" Vogel said. Michael was growing irritated, but he kept his calm and took a long swig from his beer.

"Our collective goal is to keep America strong and our enemies weak. That's one of the reasons this group was formed. One way to keep our enemies weak is to have them fight each other. One of our biggest allies in that effort was Prince Bandar of Saudi Arabia. He worked with us in 2011 and 2012 to arm the Sunnis in Iraq and encourage them to fight the Iranians, who were slowing building a land bridge across the Arabian Peninsula—a move that was a threat to Israel and a threat to the US and our allies in the Gulf.

"In partnership with Bandar and with support from the US State Department and other US intelligence agencies, we provided support to Bandar, who in turn provided support to anti-Iranian elements in Iraq and Syria. Our actions have not only been good for our respective businesses, but they also have brought sanity back to US policy in the region.

"A rogue CIA asset by the name of Pat Walsh killed Bandar. He didn't just kill him—he captured him, he tortured him and he recorded a confession that included not only Bandar's involvement in supporting those anti-Iranian forces, who are better known as ISIS, but some other very sensitive matters that would be very embarrassing to the United States if they ever got out.

"We were able to recover the recording Walsh made of Bandar's interrogation, but that was just a short-term fix. This is a dangerous guy who needed to be taken off the board permanently to prevent any future exposure and interference," said Michael.

"This is where you lose me," said Vogel, spreading his arms for affect. "Pat Walsh was in retirement in Bahamas. Why not just leave him alone? Instead, you tried to frame him by planting evidence in the Brussels bombing to make it look as though he was supplying arms to ISIS. Why do that? He had already taken himself off the board, and the attempt to frame him was simply not believable, given his background," Vogel said.

"If Walsh was off the board, the CIA director wouldn't have gone to the president of the United States to remove the sanctions against him. Walsh is a threat and he needs to be dealt with. This is the kind of thing I do every day without any of you ever knowing about it. Why are you choosing to get involved in the details now?" Michael said.

"What's done is done. Let's forget about the past. Now that you've poked the bear, what's next?" said Vogel.

"Walsh has been conducting an investigation into the Brussels bombing for the CIA. He's tracked the claymore mines used in the terrorist attack to a town near Aleppo where they were under the control of a Syrian militia group controlled by the CIA. The agent working with that group is suspected of being the person who lifted the claymores and supplied them to whoever set Walsh up.

"This agent, Fouad Zhattari, was killed yesterday by a roadside bomb in Syria. Any connections leading back to any of us have been severed. The next step is to go on the offensive and destroy Walsh. I won't tell you how I plan to do it, but a personal tragedy in his life is going to force him to quit this investigation," Michael said firmly, with conviction in his voice.

"How about we take a break and refresh our drinks, drain the lizard and then come back and continue this conversation?" Vogel said in his slow Texas drawl.

When the group returned to the porch after a fifteen-minute break, the tension was even higher than before. A number of animated sidebar conversations had taken place during the break.

"Michael, I need to be straight with you. Killing CIA employees isn't what this group is about. We were formed for altruistic reasons," said Vogel.

"That is total bullshit and you know it. We were also formed to make money. I came to you the year after I graduated with a plan for a company. When that company took off, you asked me how you could see the same growth. I showed you the benefits of leveraging my relationship with my father's people. You know who the Genovese family is, and you know what they do. When we took our methods to the world stage and began to impact the demand side of our industry, you brought in the rest of the men in this group. We have all thrived. Quit the nonsense about patriotism. This has always been about money," Michael said.

David Cohen stood up unsteadily, a tall scotch in his hand. He was the only member of the group showing any visible signs of intoxication.

"A weak Syria, a weak Iran and a weak Iraq are all good for Israel. I was totally on board with nurturing ISIS as long as they were destroyed in the end. We all agree on the strategic goals—it's the methods. I never gave my approval to kill CIA agents or to blow up hundreds of innocent people up in Western Europe. This whole thing is spiraling out of control, and it needs to stop now," David said.

Michael was at the limits of being able to control himself. He considered walking across to David Cohen and snapping his skinny neck, and, that thought relaxed him.

"We have all made a lot of money and the only guy who has ever gotten his hands dirty is me. I'll solve this problem with Walsh, the same way I have solved every other problem in the past. You guys need to relax and let me do my thing," Michael said.

"Doing your thing is placing all of us in serious jeopardy. This is what we don't understand. Why go after Pat Walsh? He seems like a guy who just wants to retire. Why not let him go instead of starting a fight we may not win? The guy is Delta Force, he's a proven survivor. Even worse, he's an assassin.

"Bandar was in hiding, in a closed-off country, in a walled compound, surrounded by guards, and Walsh snatched him, tortured him and then killed him. He did the same thing with two billionaire Arab leaders who had even better security. He isn't an hombre we want to mess with. He's an American, and he's in the same business we're in. In fact, he sells many of the products we make. We need to make peace with Walsh, not make him an enemy," said Vogel.

"I'll handle Walsh. Now that he has the scent, he won't quit investigating. Better he disappears, same as Fouad Zhattari. Nobody'll be the wiser," said Michael. While still seated, Vogel put his arm around Michael.

"All right, Michael, this is your baby. But how about after this thing with Walsh is taken care of, we go back to our regular business of winning bigger slices of a bigger pie and leave the espionage business to the professionals?" Vogel said in a conciliatory tone. Michael forced a smile, nodded and finished his beer.

Michael watched the other guys leave the porch. The men around him were weak, they were greedy, and they lacked the mental toughness needed to win a fight. He was sure that if the government ever came after him, every one of these guys would turn on him in a heartbeat. The thought caused him to realize that somebody in his organization must have already turned on him. Otherwise, Vogel would never have known so much about the actions he had taken against Pat Walsh.

When he'd started out, the funding he'd received from the Genovese family had not been enough. He also hadn't wanted to be one hundred percent indebted to the mob, which was why he'd recruited other investors like Vogel and the other members of the group. The utility of those other investors was over; they were now more of a liability.

Michael considered having all five of the men with him at the camp killed but thought it would be too risky. They were all too prominent and high-profile, and he would never get away with it. Scaring them into silence and submission was a better approach. Michael decided he would have a discussion with his uncle on the subject as soon as possible.

Chapter 10

Dubai, UAE

Pat finished tying up the *Sam Houston* to the slip in the Dubai Marina. It was a brutally hot day under the full sun. Ten minutes outside in the heat and humidity and he was already drenched in sweat as he headed toward the triple door that led into the yacht's salon. He shivered as he felt the cold blast of the air conditioning against his wet body. Summer was a difficult time to be on the water in UAE.

The sleek design of the Azimut 64 never got old for him. The deluxe interior was bright and spacious. Everything was engineered to perfection. The yacht had a sleek modern design that not only was able to handle the worst sea states but provided an unequaled level of luxury and comfort. The beige leather furniture and polished blond wood surfaces throughout the interior created a warm, relaxing ambience, which was exactly the opposite of his present mood.

The phone call from Mike Guthrie the previous night had been discouraging. His number one lead, Fouad Zhattari, the agent from Madieri whom the CIA had recalled for questioning, had been killed by a vehicle-born improvised explosive device (VBIED) at the helicopter pickup zone while he was awaiting his flight to a safe house for questioning.

The investigation was now at a dead end for Mike and Pat. The JTTF was still plugging along in Belgium, but Mike was effectively cut off, which meant Pat was as well. The director forbade Mike from allowing Pat to continue the investigation inside Belgium. The investigation had already accomplished the most important objective, which was to clear Trident of any wrongdoing, but it had accomplished little in the way of determining who was responsible for the plot. With Fouad gone, the investigation had for all practical purposes ended.

After almost five months, Pat still did not know who or what was out to get and him and he still did not know why. The thought kept him on edge. He decided to forego his sailing trip and concentrate on the business for a while. Whoever was after him was probably not going to go away on his own, so he figured it was best to go back to work and wait for the opposition, whoever they were, to make the next move.

Pat left Sam Houston and took a taxi to the Grosvenor House Hotel. Dubai Marina was an entirely man-made waterway that had been carved out of the desert. The waterfront community of high-rise buildings was three kilometers long and featured an upscale mixture of hotels, apartments, stores and office space. The marina was home to the highest concentration of Western expats in Dubai. Beyond the marina proper, ambitious architects had fashioned Venetian-style canals. The grandeur of Dubai was a testimony to the vision and drive of the Emirate's leadership, who had a genuine desire to create something special in the Middle East. Burj Khalifa was the tallest building in the world. The malls were tourist destinations with ski slopes and aquariums. The Palm was a man-made peninsula formed in the shape of a giant palm tree, and the World was a series of man-made islands crafted into the shape of a Mercator map of the globe. The over-the-top extravagance of Dubai was something that amazed Pat.

Pat walked past the Bentley dealership adjacent to the lobby and entered the hotel to meet Alexi and Max at Bar 44 on the top floor of the hotel. As he exited the elevator, he was slightly disoriented by the glare of the bright white interior and the sunlight from the huge floor-to-ceiling panoramic windows. Once he got his bearings, Pat spotted Max with his bushy Paul Bunyan beard and long curly brown hair. Alexi sat next to Max at one of the tables next to the window. Alex had white hair, intelligent grey eyes and a physique reflecting a strong affection for food and drink.

Pat was warmly greeted by both men as they shook hands and then returned to their seats. He ordered a bottle of Berringer Private Reserve chardonnay for himself and a bottle of Beluga Gold for his Russian friends. Alexi was a retired senior Russian Foreign Service officer with decades of experience working as a Russian diplomat in the US during the Cold War. He was a gifted storyteller; some of his tales stretched credulity, but they were always entertaining, and Pat felt that he came away from every meeting with a greater understanding and appreciation of the Russians.

With the sun setting and the two bottles beginning to show signs of fatigue, Pat decided it was time to talk business. Alexi had just finished a story about Leonid Brezhnev's body double meeting Senator Ted Kennedy in New York during a United Nations visit. It must have been a favorite of Alexi's, because it was the second time he had told the story to Pat. The thought of the Lion of the senate requesting help from the Russians to win the 1980 presidential election and being rewarded with a face-to-face meeting with a substitute general secretary was kind of funny, but it was yet another Alexi tale that challenged belief.

"I received your quote on the BTR-90s. My people are working on the contract," said Pat.

"It's a very good deal. The vehicles are in excellent shape," Alexi said.

"We'll conduct a technical inspection before they ship. We'll pay eighty percent on shipping documents and twenty percent when they arrive at their final destination," Pat said.

"We'll need an advance payment. We have a lot of upfront expenses on this; if we don't pay the sale could be blocked," Alexi said.

"How much of an advance?"

"Fifty percent."

"The best we can do is a thirty percent advance payment, fifty percent on shipping documents and twenty percent on final acceptance," Pat said.

"I'll talk to the them and I'll make it work," said Alexi.

"That's good. How are they going to get the vehicles into N'Djamena? Do you know what port they're planning to use? I don't think either Nigeria or Cameroon will provide clearance."

"We looked at that. We also tried Libya and Sudan, but we couldn't get guarantees. We're going to fly them in," said Alexi.

"That's a good idea. If you use an AN-225, you can probably do it in three flights."

"I don't know what they plan to use. They're a very capable company, so I'm sure it won't be a problem for them."

"Max, have you laid eyes on the stock? At forty-seven-million dollars, they need to be in perfect shape," Pat said.

"Yes, I went to Arzamas myself and saw the factory where the eight-by-eights are being refitted. They'll be like factory new," said Max.

"Where's Arzamas?"

"It's about five hundred kilometers east of Moscow. Very beautiful area, nice scenery. You should come with the technical inspection team," Max said.

"I don't want to press my luck. I'm still surprised the Russian government is allowing Arzamas to sell us the vehicles.

I'm even more surprised Rosboron Exports is letting us buy direct," said Pat.

"Russian doesn't like Boko Haram any more than the Americans. This is an area where the two countries have common cause and can cooperate," said Alexi.

"I guess. Let's just get this deal done before anyone changes their mind. *Da svidanya*, gentlemen," Pat said as he stood to leave.

Feeling slightly lightheaded as he entered the elevator for the forty-four-floor ride down, Pat reflected on how much business was done with the Russians while intoxicated. Consistency was a rare commodity in his world, and he appreciated the way the Russians stayed true to form. It was his own government he had trouble understanding.

Here he was buying eight-by-eight armored combat vehicles from our enemy Russia on behalf of the American government, to deliver to Chad, who would deploy them to Mali to fight against Boko Haram, who were being funded by our friends and allies in Saudi Arabia. Meanwhile he had ten other CIA projects where he was supplying combat equipment to fighters in Yemen and Syria who were battling Shia elements, primarily because they were a threat to Sunni Saudi Arabia. So with some actions he was working against Saudi, and in others working for Saudi.

As a bit player, barely on the fringe of US foreign policy, understanding the grand strategy was not a requirement. Still, sometimes he had to wonder if any strategy existed at all. The contradictions and inconsistencies were difficult to make sense of. Thank God for alcohol.

When Pat returned to his yacht, the sun was barely peeking above the horizon and the temperature was still in the high nineties. He went to the bar in the salon and poured a double scotch. He walked downstairs to the owner's cabin and turned on the big-screen TV to watch a replay of the Red Sox game on

MLB.com. He kicked back on his queen-sized bed, intending to watch the full game. The scotch and the slow rocking of the boat lulled Pat to sleep after only two innings.

He woke a few hours later, showered, dressed and grabbed an Uber to the Atlantis Hotel. The gargantuan hotel with its distinctive well-lit arch dominated the horizon on the three-mile drive along the entire road that extended from the base to the tip of the Palm, where the Atlantis as located. Once out of the car, he entered the doors to the hotel. He passed the many shops in the hallway filled with tourists, and beyond the aquarium, he spotted the Nobu restaurant and entered the bar. A young Filipina hostess seated Pat at a table in the back of the dark bar.

Sipping a draft Asahi beer in the dark, listening to the DJ play an eclectic mix of electronic dance and pop music while checking his emails on his iPhone, Pat was surprised to feel a warm kiss on his cheek and smell the cloying scent of perfume. He looked up to see the beautiful smiling face of Sue-Sue. Shu Xiu Wong was the Middle East sales representative for the leading Chinese government aerospace company.

"You're losing your skills, commando. I snuck right up on you," said Sue-Sue in a singsong voice.

"Do you want to join me for a drink or go right to the table?" said Pat. Sue-Sue took Pat by the arm and led him through the dark restaurant, with its walls made of swirling beads, to a table located in the center.

"You look great, Pat. Are you doing okay?" said Sue-Sue.

"I'm doing good, thanks for asking."

"Don't lie to me, I know you too well," said Sue-Sue.

Pat chuckled as the waiter brought a bowl of salted Edamame, a bottle of sparkling water for Sue-Sue and another Asahi for Pat. For the next forty-five minutes, the waiters brought a constant stream of dishes to the table, beginning with yellowfin sashimi and ending with salmon tartare and caviar.

Pat was trying to figure out how Sue-Sue was ordering, when he had yet to see a menu get delivered to the table.

Later the two were drinking cappuccino and considering desert.

"It's still early. We should go somewhere," said Pat.

"Where do you recommend?"

"Bali. We can set sail in thirty minutes."

Sue-Sue's brown eyes sparkled and the dimples showed on her cheeks as she smiled. "What about Diane?"

"I don't remember ever telling you about Diane. Besides, I met you long before Diane. I'm sure she'll understand," said Pat.

"I'm too old for you. I think you only enjoy girls half your age."

"You're the best of both worlds. You have the looks of the hottest thirty-year-old I've ever met, and you can carry on a conversation in nine languages and even order at this restaurant using some kind of telepathy. You're my ideal woman."

"I don't think the people we work with would be very happy if we had a relationship."

"It's a classic love story. Instead of Capulets and Montagues, it's USA and China. Forbidden love and all that. But instead of the dual suicide, I suggest a plot twist. Instead we sail the Pacific and drink mai tais," said Pat.

"I won't sail the Pacific with you, but I'll join you on your boat for a drink. There are some things we need to discuss in a more private setting."

Sue-Sue had a car waiting when they exited the restaurant. She told the driver where to go in Chinese. It was not a surprise to Pat that she knew where his boat was docked. She always seemed to know everything.

"I don't think you've ever been aboard the *Sam Houston* before. Do you want a tour?"

"Not right now," said Sue Sue as she sat down on the couch inside the salon. "What would you like to drink?" said Pat.

"Bourbon. Neat," said Sue Sue. Pat searched the bar for the bottle of Pappy Van Winkle Reserve he kept secured in the cabinet. The exterior lights were off in the boat and the interior was dimmed. The water was calm and the boat was gently rocking. Pat played his "Guardians of the *Galazy* album on the sound system after handing Sue-Sue her drink.

"This is really nice. I've always wanted to be seduced by you on your yacht," said Sue-Sue.

"You should have told me that years ago. We could be celebrating our fifth anniversary by now," Pat said as he sat next to Sue-Sue with his right arm around her and the drink in his left hand. "You aren't ever going to retire and move away with me, are you?"

"No. Although I would really like to."

"Why not?" said Pat.

"It isn't permitted. When I retire, I have to return to China."

"I'm okay with living in China," Pat said.

"Settling down in Beijing with a CIA agent is also not permitted," Sue-Sue said.

"I'm not an agent. You're the agent. I'm just hired labor, a contractor, not much more than a freight forwarder," Pat said.

"What was Syria like?"

"It's total chaos. ISIS is on its last legs, but there are at least a dozen factions positioning themselves to make a claim on the land and fill the vacuum once ISIS is gone."

"What were you doing there?"

"You must know someone tried to pin the Belgian bombing on me. I was tracking down the route the explosives took from when I delivered them in Iraq to how they got to Europe."

"Any luck?" said Sue-Sue.

"I lost the trail in Madeira."

"Fouad Zhattari was the CIA agent in Madeira, and he was your prime suspect. He was recalled by the CIA for questioning and was killed before he could leave Syria."

"I know," Pat said.

"Not that many people would have known Zhattari was being recalled. Only someone in the CIA would have that information."

"Are you saying the CIA had Zhattari killed? If you knew what was going on, how can you say only the CIA knew?" Pat said.

"I'm not saying the CIA killed Zhattari. I'm saying the person the CIA works for had Zhattari killed," said Sue-Sue.

"Are you accusing the president?"

"We believe it was the DNI."

"When I got shut down because of that bullshit connection to the explosives used in the terrorist attack, the CIA director and the DNI personally interceded with the president on my behalf. I've never met either the director or the DNI. It's hard to believe they would have gone to bat for me, then sent me to Syria to start an investigation, only to end it once it began to get some traction," Pat said.

"We believe the Director of National Intelligence learned of Zhattari being recalled and that the hit was done by a contract team that does black ops for the DIA," said Sue-Sue.

"You know I have to report this conversation."

"Of course, that is the whole point."

"You just ruined my dream evening, I hope you know that," Pat said as he drained his glass and took Sue-Sue's before heading over to pour them both a refill.

When Pat sat back down, he felt like he had been punched in the gut.

"What's coming? What were you sent here to warn me about?" he asked Sue-Sue. She slid over and placed Pat's head on her lap, playing with his hair for a minute while sipping her bourbon.

"There aren't permanent allies or enemies, only interests. On a personal level, you're a special friend, but on a professional level, we work together because it furthers the interest of who we work for. In some areas, we share US interests in the region. We happen to agree with your president when it comes to pursuing stability in the Middle East, and with his reluctance to commit more US forces in the region. My work with you, supplying equipment that is transferred to the Peshmerga, is a good example of how we can work together when our interests align," Sue-Sue said.

"I know that to you I'm just a dumb infantryman, but I'm following you," Pat said. Sue-Sue bent down and kissed Pat on the lips.

"Nobody is accusing you of being dumb. You and I have mutual interests. Our two countries have mutual interests. There's an element at the top of the US government that is working against the interest of your president and the people who voted him into office. Many of those interests are shared by my country, and we want you to stop them," said Sue-Sue as she lightly touched his forehead with her fingers.

Pat sat up and placed his empty glass on the coffee table. He looked at Sue-Sue. She was stunningly beautiful, with almond-shaped brown eyes and a cute button nose. He slipped his hand under her legs and stood up. At five foot seven, she weighed less than a hundred pounds, and Pat easily lifter her in a seated position with one arm around her tiny waist.

"What are you doing?" Sue-Sue said.

"Taking you downstairs," said Pat with a smile.

Pat woke early the next morning with Sue-Sue holding him tight. He reached over for the remote control to his satellite TV and turned on the TV mounted on the cabin wall, switching it to the Red Sox game. A few innings into the game, Sue-Sue began to stir. The morning light was seeping through a crack in the window curtain. Sue-Sue got out of bed and walked out of the room. Watching her return minutes later with two cups of coffee, still naked, caused Pat to take his eyes off the game, which elicited a warm smile from Sue-Sue.

"Can we finish our conversation from last night?" said Sue-Sue. Pat muted the TV and sipped his coffee.

"Sure. I think we left off at 'Baby, don't stop, oh honey, oh honey,'" said Pat.

"We want you to talk to Mike Guthrie and share the information with him," said Sue-Sue.

"That's good. I'm not cut out to be an agent, much less a double agent," said Pat.

"He trusts you and you trust me."

"I do trust you. We've done business together for years and you've always been straight with me. Plus, I've had a thing for you since forever. But what you're talking about, the accusations you're making, you need to provide some proof," said Pat.

"The attack in Belgium was a reckless move by a group within the US government who use extreme measures to create conflicts and embroil the US in foreign interventions," Sue-Sue said while balancing her coffee cup on her flat stomach. "There have always been elements within the US government who were more hawkish, but this group uses the military and intelligence agencies to further its aims."

"Without names and without proof, this isn't going to go very far," Pat said.

"The reason it isn't going to go far is because people within your government will suppress it, the same way they suppressed the information you obtained from Prince Bandar, and the same way they ended the Belgium investigation by killing Fouad Zhattari."

"Being in the weapons business, buying and selling from who I do and coordinating it with the CIA, puts me under the microscope of a lot of agencies that collect information on me. It seems everyone listens to my phone calls. It's not that small of a group that would have known about Bandar and Zhattari. Case in point, you knew about Zhattari," said Pat.

"It's a small group—only the CIA knew about both, yet in both cases other agencies within the US became involved and destroyed evidence," said Sue-Sue.

"You know about how they took the Bandar interrogation tapes from me."

"Of course, that was a nasty bump on the head you got."

"Bandar and those two other guys were funding ISIS from the very beginning. In their own way of thinking, they were patriots for creating armed opposition to the unrestrained growth of Iran across Arabia. I can believe Americans could see some benefit in using the caliphate crazies to undermine Iran. But the attack in Brussels makes no sense at all. Why would any American want something like that to happen?"

"Defense spending. ISIS has been almost completely destroyed in Iraq and Syria. Once that happens, many will believe the war against ISIS is over. Moving the war to Europe will make sure the elevated defense spending remains," Sue-Sue said.

"You're saying it's China's position that there's a cabal in the US government that is fomenting war for commercial reasons?"

"Partly, yes. And we wouldn't have detected it if it weren't for you. You more or less stumbled into this when you were attacked. You hunted down Prince Bandar, Sheik Meshal and Sheik Rasheed, which ended most of the GCC funding for ISIS. The US covered up most of what you discovered, and then they set you up with the Brussels bombing. Tying you to that attack as a way to shut you down was a mistake. They have overreached. You weren't a threat—you were semi-retired in Bahamas with your pretty surfer girl. They went too far again by pushing for sanctions against you and by killing Fouad Zhattari," said Sue-Sue.

"That makes sense. The few facts we know fit the story. Just tell me who's involved and I'll track these guys down and give them the same treatment the GCC leaders got," Pat said.

"We don't know who's involved. My superiors asked me to pass this information to you, so you would pass it to Mike Guthrie. We want you to root out this element within your government. They're a danger to both our countries' interests. Our hope is that you continue your investigation and that you proceed with caution, because there are definitely elements within the CIA working against you."

"The investigation is pretty much at a dead end with the death of Zhattari," Pat said.

"Your president ran for office as an isolationist. Look closely at the events and the people who have influenced him to reverse his position."

"I'll talk to Mike and let him figure this out. You should come with me. We can be a team," said Pat. Sue-Sue began to gently kiss Pat on the neck and then gradually moved lower.

"I'll assist where I can, but I think its best if you avoid distraction," said Sue-Sue while removing the covers from his body.

Chapter 11

Duck, Outer Banks, North Carolina

Pat watched from inside the black Tahoe as the Gulfstream G550 taxied to the end of the airstrip and stopped near the lone building at the aircraft turnaround area. Once the stairs were in place, he drove the SUV to the aircraft and stopped at the base. A lone passenger descended the stairs, wearing sunglasses, beige shorts and a white PFD fishing shirt. Pat exited the driver's side to greet him.

"How was your flight, Mike?" said Pat.

"Only twenty-five minutes from Potomac Airfield. On a busy weekend like this, it would take seven hours to drive with the traffic on Route 12." Mike threw his bag in the backseat and hopped into the passenger seat.

"That's the gym over there," Pat said, pointing out the building at the near end of the airstrip. "Behind those trees, they have clay tennis courts. I have racquets in case you're interested in playing. There's a golf course down the road too. It's called the Curritak Club. We have a tee time at nine a.m. tomorrow."

They drove through the Pine Island neighborhood entrance and parked in circular driveway of one of the many oceanfront homes. "There are a bunch of bedrooms upstairs.

One of the oceanfront ones with balcony access is open," said Pat.

While Mike unpacked, Pat filled a small cooler with six bottles of Little Hump Spring Ale and grabbed a couple of bags of chips and moved out onto the second-floor deck overlooking the ocean. Several minutes later, Mike slipped into the beach chair.

"This is all very bromantic, Pat. Now why the hell am I here on my weekend, when I should be home barbequing with the family?"

Pat opened the cooler, withdrew a beer, opened it with a bottle opener, placed it in a cozy and handed it to Mike. He tossed a bag of Tostados lime chips at him.

"Have some of that Little Hump and settle down. If I could have told you what I know over a secure line, I would have. By the way, I rented two surfboards. High tide is tomorrow at six forty, and there's a storm offshore that's kicking up some decent swells."

"I don't surf, I don't play tennis and I don't golf," said Mike.

"I remember when you did all those things. What happened to those good old days, when we were in the hooah battalion and you knew how to enjoy life?"

"Well, I got shot three times in Honduras, for one thing. Then I fell into a ravine during Delta selection and broke my leg in two places. Now my arthritis has arthritis and I work a hundred and five hours a week."

"You should have said something. I never even noticed a limp. You know, I remember finding you bleeding out on that trail after you earned your Purple Heart—I mean, enemy marksmanship award—in Hondo. I thought you were just sniveling. I had to carry you all the way back to base camp. And at selection they told us you were a motivational drop. LOM—Lack of Motivation. They said you quit because you couldn't watch Oprah. I had no idea you fell down and hurt yourself. You're carrying around a lot of emotional pain. You may want to talk to someone about that. Tell you what, while I surf and golf tomorrow, I'll order you a massage to get all that Potomac poison out of your system. Sanderling Hotel is a five-star and it's right down the street. I'll bet they have an outstanding spa," said Pat.

The two men drank their beer and looked out at the empty beach. The waves were breaking loud with a crash, the seagulls squawking as they raced from the oncoming surf. They could taste and smell the salt air brought in from the coastal breeze, and in the twilight, they could see dark clouds on the horizon.

"I'm going to take you up on that offer," said Mike. The two men sat quietly, each finishing his beer and opening a second one.

"Are you ready to talk shop?" said Pat.

"Send it," said Mike.

"I met Colonel Shu Xiu Wong three nights ago in Dubai. We had dinner at Nobu in Atlantis. She's still amazingly beautiful. The dinner was terrific. They do this thing with salmon tartare and caviar that deserves an award. Anyway, we went back to my boat after and had drinks. You know the Chinese keep up with me pretty close. We use them for stuff we can't get licensed from USA and Europe. You pay the bills, so you know they provided us the radar and ADA systems last year for the Kurds. The relationship has always been good, and of course I've always had the hots for Sue-Sue. She's fifty and looks like Lucy Liu did at twenty-five. She's my kryptonite. We had a long night. It was life-changing. I hoped she was there because of me, but what I learned was that she was working, and the real reason she met with me was because she had a message for you."

"That has got to be the longest and most profoundly disturbing preamble to an intelligence report in CIA history," said Mike.

"I want you to understand the context. Sue-Sue and I have a relationship. She's always had orders to keep things professional. It's significant that this was the first time her overseers give her the opportunity to spend personal time with me, and what does she do? She jumps my bones. That has to mean something. You have to know that to understand the context," said Pat.

"I'm not really sure that I do, but I get that you trust her, and that is something she would consider."

"Definitely. Plus, she knows whatever she tells me, I'm going to relay to you. She also knows that when people try to play with me and lie, I tend to get violent."

"Maybe that's why the Chinese used a girl you have schoolboy crush on, instead of someone you would toss off a building. Anyway, let's get to the point. What was her message for me?" Mike asked.

"Chinese intelligence believes there's a group of senior US government officials in defense and intelligence who are running a shadow foreign policy. They think this group was working with Bandar, Meshal and Rasheed. They also think these guys were responsible for the disappearance of Bandar's taped confession. The Chinese believe this secret group is responsible for the Belgium bombing and for attempting to frame me," Pat said.

"Any evidence?"

"Not much. She said the death of Fouad Zhattari is proof, because only the CIA knew he was being recalled for questioning. She said the DNI knew about the recall order and that a DIA contract hit team did the job. She said the president was an isolationist six months ago, but because events are being orchestrated by these guys to influence his position, he's become a hawk. She said in addition to the manipulation of events, there are people working with this secret group who are close to the president, influencing him. She believes the group is motivated by greed and by patriotism."

"Why did she say she was helping us?" Mike said.

"She said it was in both of our countries' interest to stop this group before they start a major shooting war," said Pat.

"You've had a few days to think about this. What's your take on it all?"

"A secret cabal of bad guys bent on world domination and getting rich inside the defense industry is a sort of unifying theory that explains a lot of things that have been happening lately. We were already more or less investigating this without Chinese intervention. I think the only reason they talked to me was they wanted to warn us to keep the circle tight because not everyone in the intelligence community can be trusted."

"Another possibility is they may want to sic Pat Walsh the wild man against our own people. Damage our capabilities by triggering you to do the same thing to selected US intel leaders that you did to those Arab malefactors, which was basically to hunt them down and kill them in spectacular fashion," Mike said.

"I don't think Sue-Sue would set me up that way."

"You're smitten. Where she's concerned, I don't think you're thinking with your head."

"There may have been one point during our evening when I offered the nuclear launch codes if she stayed longer, but otherwise I was pretty nonchalant about the whole thing," Pat said.

"Do you have any ideas on how to move forward with this information?"

"I'm just going to sit here, watch the sun set, drink many more of these aptly named Little Hump Beers and reflect upon my most intimate moments with the famous Sue-Sue, the Mata

Hari of the modern spy era. I'm going to take your lead on this. Obviously, somebody in your shop is a traitor, but unless you give me the green light I'm not going to snatch anyone off the street or do anything radical," Pat said.

"Zhattari getting killed was no coincidence. This is inside stuff that could cause serious problems if mishandled. Nothing personal, but you aren't an agent, you're a contractor. The director won't like that the Chinese went to you," Mike said.

"How could I forget I'm not an agent, Michael? I'm like Dwight Schutte. Every time I try to tell people I'm the assistant regional manager, you follow behind to remind me that I'm the assistant to the regional manager—an asset, not agent," Pat said with a chuckle.

"Keep this between us, and tread carefully. I need to go to the director with this. Do you mind if I borrow your rental truck?" said Mike as he stood up.

"What about all the beer I bought? And tomorrow's massage? I haven't even given you the details on the awesomeness that is Sue-Sue. Are you really going to walk out on that?" Pat said.

"This can't wait. I'll just have to wait for the movie. It's a shame the title *Beauty and the Beast* has already been taken," Mike said.

Chapter 12

New York City

Michael Genovese rotated around the bed and tested the knots with his hands. He paid special attention to make sure they were tight enough to prevent escape, but not so tight they cut off circulation. He used rainbow-colored 9mm kernmantle from REI and was confident in the quality of his work. Anika, this week's internet catch, was a fashion model—a thin, dark-haired Latvian beauty. The terrified young woman was positioned facedown and naked on the bed. Her mouth was muzzled with a ball Michael had found in an S&M shop, and her limbs were tied in a spread-eagle position. Tears streamed down her face, her eyes were swollen and bloodshot, and her face was red from exertion as she struggled futilely against the restraints.

"I have to take a meeting, sweetheart. I'll be back just as soon as I can," said Michael as he shut off the lights and left the room.

Michael met Nicky Terranova at the elevator entry to his penthouse apartment. Nicky was in his late sixties, six feet tall and rail thin, with a prominent Sicilian nose. The two men shook hands. Michael mixed an old-fashioned for Nicky and poured a Red Bull for himself before he led the older man out onto the terrace. Standing at the rail overlooking Central Park, the two men quietly observed the greenery sixty floors below.

"Your father would be proud of what you have accomplished," said Nicky.

"I'm just getting started," Michael said.

"You're a smart kid. What you're doing is impressive. My cousin sees you as the future." Barney Bellomo was Nicky's second cousin and the head of the Genovese Mafia.

"His investment in G3 has made him a very wealthy man. His faith was not misplaced."

"No, it wasn't. But don't get too cocky. Let's face it, without his support, you'd be living in a duplex on Long Island," Nicky said.

"I doubt that, Nicky, but I get what you're saying. Let Barney know from me that I'm appreciative. I'm in his debt."

"Mitch Vogel came to see me the other day."

"What did he want?" Michael asked.

"Nothing, really. He was just feeling around, trying to get information on the internal workings of our shareholders' agreement."

"He's a minority shareholder without even a place on the board. What does he want with that?"

"I'm thinking he was testing to see how secure your control was."

"Anybody else want to see me replaced?" Michael asked.

"Nope, he's the only one, and he never came out and said it. He was just testing the waters."

"Mitch is an old man. He's at that age where he's worried about his legacy. He's having a bit of amnesia about how he got to where he is."

"We need to continue this conversation inside," Nicky said.

Michael fixed Nicky a second drink and the two men sat in the windowless theater room. Michael turned on the Yankees game, which was in the seventh inning in the waning part of the afternoon. In the eighties, Barney Bellomo had beaten a murder charge, but he'd spent twelve years in prison on a RICO conviction that had been obtained through wiretaps. Ever since then, business communication had always been done in person, preferably in a room routinely swept for bugs, without windows and with all cell phones left outside the room.

"We hired a guy for that request you made. He took the contract, then came back a week later and demanded double," Nicky said.

"You should find someone else. Guy sounds like a crook."

"It's more than one guy. It's an organization from Macedonia—very expensive, but very good. We had to outsource because your guy travels so much. We don't have that kind of reach. Your problem should be solved soon."

"That's good," Michael said.

"Barney is asking what kind of problem requires three hundred and fifty thousand to eliminate. He thinks he should know about something that serious," Nicky said.

"Pat Walsh is an international arms dealer. He works mostly US government contracts, and he's looking into things that are best not looked into. He doesn't even know who I am, but he needs to disappear before he learns anything.".

"Good enough for me. I'm sure it'll be the same for the boss."

Michael walked Nicky to the elevator.

"What are you doing tonight? Do you want to go for dinner?" said Nicky.

"I can't, I already made plans."

"Hot date tonight? Taking a lady out on the town?"

"Just a romantic dinner at the apartment. Who knows? Maybe tonight I'll get lucky. Are you planning on coming to the house for the Labor Day barbeque?"

"I wouldn't miss it," Nicky said. "Last year was fantastic. The live band, the food, the fireworks—you and your brothers really know how to throw a bash, and it's always good to see the kids."

Michael closed and locked the door behind Nicky. On his way to the master bedroom, he became distracted by the floor-length mirror in the hallway. He removed his shirt and practiced some flexes and poses before moving along the hallway with a smile.

Chapter 13

Outer Banks, North Carolina

The raindrops were big and heavy as they fell against his back and shoulders. His arms were wind-milling as he thrust the surfboard over the water with his powerful strokes. The wave was a bomb, the biggest of the day. He felt the surf propel the board on the drop, and he quickly sprang up into a backside position with ageless agility. Gliding downward to the base of the wave, he shifted his weight and executed a bottom turn and angled left.

He was able to execute four fast climbing and dropping maneuvers before he felt the break of the wave on top of his head and had to bail. Standing in the waist-deep water to retrieve his surfboard, he looked toward the house and saw a man standing under the awning on the second-floor porch, applauding.

The distance was too great to tell if the man was Mike, but he assumed it was and took his return as his cue to quit for the day. He placed his board under his arm and fought the surf back to the house.

"How's the surfing?" Mike said.

"For the Outer Banks, it's about as good as it gets," Pat said.

"Surfing in the rain during a thunderstorm looks like a pretty good way to die."

"That lightning is at least ten miles out. I was paying attention."

"Why don't you take a shower and dress? I'll make some coffee."

Pat returned in a pair of jeans and a Furman University baseball T-shirt. Mike was seated at the table, scrolling through emails on his CIA-issued smartphone.

"What did you learn from our political masters?" Pat asked.

"I met with the director and with the DNI."

"The DNI?" said Pat in a quizzing tone.

"The guy that does the daily brief to the president is the DNI. He's also the guy in charge of the assets that operate domestically. He had to be brought in. Your Asian crush who happens to work for our archenemies suggesting the DNI may be playing for the wrong team doesn't exactly reach the level of proof needed to violate my oath of office. The director insisted we keep the DNI in the loop," Mike said.

"I understand. That stuff is in your lane. What did the big guys think?"

Mike got up and walked to the kitchen counter and returned with the coffeepot. Without asking, he topped off Pat's cup and refilled his own.

"They think it's a theory worth looking into. The two leads we have are the Brussels bombing and the murder of Fouad Zhattari. I'm sending a team to Syria to look into what Zhattari was up to in Syria and how he died. I'm sending you to Belgium to link up with the team from the Joint Terrorism Task Force to work the problem from that end," Mike said.

"I thought you didn't want me in Belgium."

"This was the director's call. Normally my assets are restricted to the MENA region, but this is very closely held, and we want to read in as few people as possible. If you're still game, he wants you to go to Belgium," Mike said.

"No objections from my end. Did you learn anything that might be useful on the progress of the Brussels investigation," Pat asked.

"They haven't found much. They have only one decent lead. They're trying to locate a woman who was near the square, at a table in the Hard Rock Café with Eleiwi the bomber, but they haven't been able to find her in Brussels."

"I'll track her down," Pat said.

"That's the confidence we need."

"I guess this means I finally made the team. Agent Walsh, I like it."

"Our lone agent on the ground attached to the JTTF team is Natalia De'Levaga. She won't like you, so try not to annoy her too much. I'll get you her contact info so you can meet once you arrive. She's been instructed to update you on the status of the investigation and what they know about this mystery woman, who we believe has disappeared into the Brussels Muslim community. Put your unique skill set to use and track the woman down and learn what you can," Mike said.

"What about weapons and logistics support?"

"You're on your own. Call me when you learn something," Mike said.

Chapter 14

Brussels, Belgium

Pat spent the morning walking around the Grand Place Square. The day was slightly overcast with temperatures in the high seventies. The square was filled with tourists. From the café, next to the town hall, he could see craftsmen restoring the gothic façade of a building on the opposite side of the square that must have borne the brunt of the explosion. All of the evidence of the destructive blast had been swept from the cobblestones. The concussive blast would have broken many of the windows inside the small enclosed square, but he didn't notice a single window still in need of repair.

Security inside the square consisted of four stationary soldiers posted in each corner, more of a deterrent than anything else. Near where the craftsman was restoring the façade, there was a large makeshift memorial against a wall. Teddy bears, ribbons and candles were all arranged in remembrance of the victims. Nothing wrong with honoring the fallen, Pat thought, but it was going to take more than sympathetic Facebook posts, teddy bears and a good cleaning crew to eliminate the problem.

Pat walked to the southeast corner of the square and entered the Hard Rock Café. He told the hostess he was looking for a friend who was already seated and was ushered inside. He spotted the security cameras in the entryway at the second- and third-floor stairway entrances. Inside the restaurant on the third floor, he toured the dining room. The room had a bar against the inside wall. Across from the bar was a glass-enclosed picture drawn by John Lennon. It was just a large piece of paper with a big circle drawn on it and small dot in the middle of the circle, with "we are here" written next to the dot. The picture seemed to get a lot of attention from the dining tourists. Apparently, it was evidence of creative genius.

On the other side of the room were large picture windows facing the square. A camera in the exterior wall corner covered the tables positioned next to the picture windows. There was another area, behind a support column, that was blocked from view of the corner camera but was in full view of the camera behind the bar. It was only noon and the restaurant was completely full.

Pat walked out of the Hard Rock. The square has six roads leading into it, and he walked onto Rue Charles and headed southwest to the Amigo Hotel, located less than a quarter mile down the road. The hotel was easy to spot. It was an appealing five-story structure with red brick exterior walls and colorful hanging flowerpots below each window. Pat entered the lobby elevator and went up to the fifth floor. He knocked on the door to room 507 and waited for Natalia De'Lavega, the woman Mike Guthrie was sure would not like him, to answer the door.

"Please come in," said Natalia in English with a Spanish accent. Natalia looked to be in her early forties. She was a well-coiffed woman with long black hair and an unblemished Mediterranean complexion. Her makeup, jewelry and impeccable black pantsuit indicated she was a woman who devoted a lot of resources to her appearance. Although not overweight, she carried a few extra pounds that no doubt must have been a struggle for her. She displayed no facial expression when he entered the room. With a sweep of her arms, she gestured to one of the two seats in the room.

Natalia sat unspeaking in the opposite seat in the living room area of the suite. After thirty seconds of uncomfortable silence, Pat decided to break the stalemate.

"I'm Pat Walsh. Mike told me you would read me in on what you have so far on the mystery woman." Natalia picked up the lone file that was sitting on the coffee table between them and slid it over to his side. Pat picked up the file and opened it. The file consisted of eleven sheets of paper, seven of them photographs taken from security footage in the Hard Rock. The photos showed them entering and leaving separately. They showed Ahmed entering without a bag and leaving with a large diaper bag on his shoulder, and they showed them sitting at the window table together from two different angles. One photo showed the woman moving behind the structural support wall with the baby and something else in her hands moments before the explosion. The still photo of the explosion showed the windows blowing in, showering the restaurant patrons with glass.

Pat spent five minutes carefully reading the four written pages and then returned the file folder to the coffee table.

"Can I keep the photos?" said Pat.

"Yes, keep the file," said Natalia.

"How did she get to the Grand Place?" said Pat.

"We don't know."

"Would you know if it was by train?"

"Yes."

"Would you know if it was by taxi?" said Pat.

"No."

"There are cameras on all the entrances to the square. Which street did she use to enter?"

"Rue de Chapelries," said Natalia.

"And you don't have anything else showing her route to the Hard Rock?" Pat asked.

"No."

"What about her egress?"

"We don't have anything."

"That's impossible. That explosion wouldn't have affected the cameras leading out of the square, and the woman was either carrying a baby or had a baby carriage. What could be easier to spot?"

"The JTTF has been working closely with the Belgian Police and Interpol. All the agencies have many years of experience in these matters. If you think you can do better, then feel free to try," Natalia said.

Pat couldn't tell if Natalia was really upset. Her words had a hard edge to them, but her face showed nothing.

"Do you have any other information you think will be useful in helping me find this woman?" he asked.

"No."

"I'll be sure to relay to Mike and the director how helpful you've been. Thanks." Pat got up and left without another word passing between them.

He walked to the Marriott, which was another five hundred meters west of the Amigo hotel and the closest decent hotel to the Molenbeek neighborhood. Molenbeek was home to the largest immigrant population in Brussels. It was from this direction that the mystery woman had entered the Hard Rock. Pat thought he'd made a wise choice in picking the hotel, because it seemed inevitable the investigation would start in Molenbeek. Back in the room, he reviewed the information provided so reluctantly by Natalia and decided to go to the gym to clear his head.

The gym at the Marriot was basic. They didn't have any free weights, so he used the machines and then hopped on the treadmill. Pat liked to think he did some of his best thinking when he ran. He was hoping a little exercise would jar a better plan out than what he had been able to come up with so far.

Molenbeek was the jihadi capital of Europe. According to one of the documents in the file, the Belgian police believed fifty-one terrorist-linked organizations operated out of the area. Unless more information surfaced, Pat's plan was to find the top guy in each of those fifty-one organizations listed in the documents Natalia had provided and interrogate them one at a time. Eventually, he figured one of the captured subjects would identify the woman.

He figured each subsequent capture would become progressively more difficult. The bad guys weren't going to go willingly, and after the first one or two, they would know what was coming and prepare defenses. He figured the Belgian police wouldn't be too thrilled with his plan either, but he didn't see them as a threat. They must have surrendered a long time ago to have allowed fifty-one terrorist-affiliated groups to operate in their own backyard.

It was going to take a lot more firepower than the lone SIG 226 9mm pistol he currently had in his hotel room safe. The first order of business was going to be securing the proper weapons and equipment.

When he got back to his room, Pat had a hard time opening his iPhone because the system couldn't read his sweaty thumb. His call finally got through to Natalia.

"I have an urgent request," said Pat.

"What is it?" said Natalia.

"I need the names and contact information of the top people in all fifty-one of those terrorist-affiliated organizations you listed in the document you gave me," said Pat.

"I need to clear that with management," said Natalia.

"Get it cleared and notify me when it's ready," said Pat. Less than an hour later, Natalia called back and notified Pat that the document would be ready for pickup at 9 p.m. that evening. The plan was to meet in the outside seating area of Scott's Bar at the corner of Rue de L'Ecuyer and Warmoesberg.

When he dressed for dinner, he added one of the three concealed armor vests he had brought with him. The very expensive soft armor vests fit like an undershirt and were lightweight, breathable and not the least bit bulky. He had a small flat vacuum-sealed first aid kit placed between the t-shirt fabric and the soft armor layer in the back of each vest. Pat carried his pistol in a shoulder holster and strapped a boot knife to his right leg. He wore jeans, boots and a navy-blue windbreaker to cover the shoulder holster containing his SIG 226 pistol and one extra magazine. He was dressed for battle, because immediately after receiving the list from Natalia, he intended to go into Molenbeek and begin reconnaissance on his first target.

He ate dinner at a small Thai restaurant near his hotel. He had missed lunch, and the Tom Yon Kai Soup and Pad Thai noodles both hit the spot. He drank green tea, knowing it was going to be a long night and alcohol would only make him sleepy. At a little after eight, he left the restaurant to meet Natalia. The sun was low in the sky and the shadows inside the city were long. Traffic was high, and Pat kept with the flow of the pedestrian traffic, which was fairly sparse. He'd learned when he'd googled it that the distance to the bar was seven hundred meters. He planned on arriving at least fifteen minutes early to scout the location.

Pat walked down the Rue de L'Ecuyer with the spire of St. Michael's Cathedral as a landmark on the horizon. Rue de L'Ecuyer was a main avenue with four lanes and wide sidewalks. Parked cars lined both sides of the road as he approached the intersection. He could hear rock music from a live band playing at the bar. He noticed the four people waiting at the bus stop and shifted his attention to the intersection as he moved. He registered movement from a parked car to his front, but before he could react, a sledgehammer-like blow hit him in the chest, and he felt his knees buckle as he fell backwards. As he fell, a second massive blow hit him in the left shoulder.

Partially stunned, lying flat on his back, he slipped his right hand into his half-zipped windbreaker and withdrew the SIG. His heart was racing and the adrenaline was spiking his system. He sat up in time to see two men with pistols drawn, fast-walking toward him while engaging. He rapid-fired, pulling the trigger three times and hitting the man to his right, who had closed to within twenty meters. He felt another huge impact to his chest, but with his left arm braced against the ground, he was able to remain upright long enough to engage the man on his left with three quick shots. After seeing the second man go down, Pat rolled over, and with the help of a building wall he was able to pull himself upright. He staggered over to the two prostrate men with his weapon drawn.

When he got to within five meters of the downed attackers, he was stuck by yet another powerful blow to his back and his right thigh, which sent him sprawling face forward toward the cement. While still descending, he rotated his body clockwise and engaged the third shooter, who was running toward him. With his vision collapsing due to the shock, Pat half-blindly fired all nine rounds remaining in his pistol at the blurred figure and didn't stop pulling the trigger until the slide locked back in place.

Crawling on his hands and knees, he moved to the first two shooters. He felt for a pulse and searched their pockets. Both were dead, and neither had any identification. He crawled over to the wall, pulled himself up and wobbled over to the third shooter. Pat was grateful to find the man alive. Shot badly in both legs and in the stomach, the man was barely conscious.

The man appeared to be a European. He was dressed in a dark blue business suit, white shirt and tie. A suppressed 9mm H&K handgun was lying within reach, and he looked to be in his mid- to late thirties. Pat kicked the pistol out of the man's reach.

"Who sent you?"

The man stared back, unresponsive. Pat slowly stuck his still empty pistol into the gaping hole of the man's stomach wound and pressed.

"Who sent you?"

The man screamed something in a Slavic-sounding language. Pat pressed harder.

"Goran Pandev. I work for Thomas Kriss," the man screamed.

"Thomas Kriss from Switzerland," Pat said, recognizing the name. The man stared back at him with lifeless eyes. Pat retrieved his pistol, released the magazine and replaced it with his spare.

Pat could hear the police sirens. Under the glare of a gathering crowd he ducked into a narrow alley between a bank and a dress shop and picked up the pace as fast as his wounds would allow. The bullet wound to his leg was bleeding badly and the blood loss was starting to make him dizzy. He removed his belt and fashioned a tourniquet above the wound and continued to move. As he emerged from the alley onto another street, he saw a man opening his car door. Pat closed the distance to the man while unholstering his pistol. He pointed the weapon at the man's face and demanded the terrified driver's keys. The man put the keys on the roof and ran. Pat staggered awkwardly into the driver's compartment and sped off in a silver Peugeot 301.

The wound in his right thigh was still bleeding badly, the improvised tourniquet working poorly. The throbbing pain was growing more intense, and he felt a sharp, stinging pain every time he inhaled. The adrenaline was wearing off, and Pat was worried he was about to lose consciousness while still on the road. He spotted a nearby parking garage and ducked in. He stayed on the up ramp until he reached the highest level and then parked in a poorly lit corner, away from any other cars.

Under an almost unbearable amount of pain, he removed his windbreaker, his shirt and his soft armor vest. He ripped open the first aid kit and removed the Celox gauze. The blood from his upper thigh was pooling in the car's leather seat. He raised himself and pulled his pants down to inspect the wound. The entry wound in the back of the thigh was small, but the exit wound on the front was the size of a quarter. He stuffed the hemostatic dressing as far inside as he could, first into the exit wound, and then, once his strength returned again, into the entrance wound. The nerves in his thigh were on fire, and tears were streaming down his face. He pressed down on the bigger wound with the palm of his right hand for a full minute, using the dashboard digital clock to keep the time. He wrapped his thigh with regular gauze and taped it tight. He pulled his blood-soaked jeans back up, reclined the seat as far back as it would go, and promptly passed out.

When he regained consciousness, it was night. He could see the half-moon out of the partially fogged windshield. He slowly powered the seat to an upright position and turned on the interior lights. He used the sun visor mirror to inspect his naked chest. The bruising from the three bullets stopped by the vest in the front was not as bad as he'd expected. Each bruise was the size of his palm and was a dark bluish black with a fading green around the edges. He felt a sharp pain when he breathed, but he didn't think any of his ribs were broken. He gingerly replaced his shirt, holster and jacket, and after unsticking himself from the bloody leather seat, he stepped out of the car. Feeling guilty for terrorizing the car owner, he withdrew his wallet and placed two thousand euros above the sun visor before locking the keys inside the car.

It was a stiff and painful hobble to the garage elevator. He inspected his reflection in the elevator doors and determined that he wouldn't draw too much unwanted attention in public. The dark jeans masked the congealing bloodstains in his pants, and the three holes in his windbreaker and black shirt were undetectable as long as the holes in the jacket and shirt weren't aligned. He had cleaned the blood from his hands using all the alcohol wipes in his first aid kit. He thought he looked presentable enough to take a taxi and walk through his hotel lobby.

While in the taxi, he took stock of the situation. The ambush he'd walked into must have required some knowledge of the route he was using, or at least the general direction he was coming from. Going back to his hotel room was a risk, but he didn't have any other options. He stopped the taxi two hundred meters short of the hotel and got out. He checked the area for surveillance before walking to the hotel and entering the lobby. He walked as normally as he could for the benefit of the cameras and was lucky to find himself alone in the elevator. He entered his room with his weapon drawn, but found it to be empty. He took a hot shower, redressed his leg wound, took 800 milligrams of Motrin and a 250-milligram Zithromax capsule and went to sleep for the next twelve hours.

Figuring the greatest likelihood of getting caught was within the first few hours, he took a chance and remained in his room recovering for the next five days. He left the hotel room only once per day to allow housekeeping to clean. He was tempted to call Mike but decided it was best to keep the CIA in the dark about his whereabouts and his plans.

The hunt for the mystery woman was going to have to wait; his new target was Thomas Kriss. Pat had met Thomas on several occasions. They had never actually done business, but they were both in the arms business, and they had discussed the possibility of working together. Thomas was a manufacturer of weapons and ammunition. Most of his factories were in Macedonia, but two of the more popular brand-named companies were in Switzerland. During the Balkans war, Kriss had made a fortune selling Cold War-stock Eastern European small arms ammunition and hardware to both the Serbs and the Bosnians.

It seemed likely Kriss was now offering training and security services, as so many of the other companies in the industry did. The problem with having a bunch of ex-special forces types on the payroll for training and personal protection services was that it was an easy step to branch into shadier lines of business that used the same skill sets. Knowing Thomas's reputation, Pat had little difficulty accepting that he'd crossed the line into the guns-for-hire business. He couldn't think of any reason Thomas would go after him, which meant he had most likely been hired to do the job. The next task was going to be finding out who had hired him and why. Despite the still nagging pain from his ordeal, it was a relief to finally have a real lead that he could pursue to unlock this mystery that had been plaguing him for months.

Chapter 15

Zurich, Switzerland

Pat boarded the Cessna Citation X jet with a small leather bag over his shoulder. The two large suitcases containing his equipment were being loaded by the ground crew. Trident maintained a hangar and storage space in Paphos, Cyprus, as a backup to the main operations in Abu Dhabi, and the personnel from XOJET Air charters were familiar with his company's obsessive demands for discretion. Pat stored most of his personal tactical equipment, weapons and ammunition in the Paphos warehouse. Although his bags would withstand a cursory search by customs without revealing any prohibited firearms, he couldn't afford to raise any suspicion that would lead the inspectors to dig deeper and find the hidden compartments within his luggage. The Brioni suit, Patek Philippe watch and ostentatious eight-passenger jet would hopefully project a law-abiding businessman persona to the customs agents, instead of his true raison d'être.

Thomas had an office in Zurich and a home thirty minutes south of the city center in Kilchberg. Pat checked in at the Widder Hotel on Reinweg Strasser because the office suite Thomas leased in Zurich was nearby on the same road. The hotel was built by connecting the interiors of nine adjacent, distinctly different townhouses. The oldest townhome was from the twelfth century, the newest from the nineteenth century. The building was unlike the many boring sterile hotels in Zurich with cold walls and hard furniture. The modern contemporary interior of Widder was warm, comfortable and relaxing. Pat instantly loved it.

After two days of unproductive surveillance of Kriss's office, Pat reluctantly decided it was time to focus on the house. He was going to miss the Widder. The restaurants were fantastic, and the Widder Bar had a list of whiskeys like none he had ever seen. Each day at 6 p.m., Pat found himself in the Widder Bar, receiving a tutorial on the various whiskeys from Wolfgang, the head bartender. Last night's Ardbeg 1978 had been a real treat. Pat hated the idea of checking out of the hotel before he had a chance to finish his education.

Thomas lived in a very nice home on lake Zurich. The two-story single residence was L-shaped and had a beautiful lawn that gently sloped down to the edge of Lake Zurich. Moored less than one hundred meters from the home was a lovely well-kept twenty-one-foot sailboat. At the edge of Thomas's lakefront property was a small landing where he kept a rowboat and a sailboard. Pat eyed the home and the property from the aptly name Seestrasse. After two passes in his rental car on the busy road, he decided to look for a place that could serve as an observation point and a base of operations.

Pat moved to a hotel across the lake from Thomas's home. Romantik Seehotel was not directly across from Thomas's home; it was at more of an oblique angle. Because Thomas's property jutted out into the lake, it allowed Pat to have a clear view from his second-story room. The distance to the house was two and a half kilometers, according to the laser range finder on his Steiner M830r binoculars. Pat accepted the room after verifying that he would have a lake view and that the double windows in his room opened. If the weather cooperated and stayed in the sixty- to seventy-degree range, he felt he would have found the perfect eagle's nest.

He unpacked the gear from both suitcases and set up the Kateye system on a tripod inside his room. Thermals didn't work well through glass, which was why being able to open the double glass doors was essential. The Kateye was a remote-controlled observation platform with both day and thermal optics. It allowed Pat to lie on his bed, or on the couch, and watch Thomas on the hotel room's big-screen TV. He was able to zoom in on a narrow field of view that allowed him to recognize faces, or he could zoom out and capture the entire home in a single picture.

Pat observed the house for three full days and nights. On two of those days, he observed Thomas rowing out to his sailboat alone, and then taking a two- to three-hour sail around the long, narrow lake. The one day he didn't sail, the weather was bad, with thunderstorms and high winds. He checked the weather forecast and decided it was time to stop watching and start moving.

It was two in the morning when he left the hotel carrying a large waterproof bag over his shoulder. The temperature outside was a chilly fifty degrees, and the cold air created goose bumps as he hurriedly stripped and put on the sleeveless wetsuit he had purchased earlier in the day at the triathlete sports store in downtown Zurich. He sealed the floating stuff bag and attached the line to his waist. He put on his swim goggles and slowly walked into the water, trailing the hydrodynamic bag with his clothes and gear. When the water reached his chest, he leaned forward and became horizontal. The water was icy cold, and it took a full minute until the water absorbing into his 5mm neoprene suit became warm enough to retain the heat of his body. He instantly regretted not buying the suit with sleeves as he began the 2.4-kilometer swim to Thomas's sailboat.

Visibility was good, the sky was clear and the moon was three-quarters full. He was able to use the lights from Thomas's house for his bearing when he lifted his head out of the water every few minutes. His ribs still hurt from the bruising they'd received in Brussels, and the thigh wound was burning with every kick. The wind gave the lake a small chop, throwing water into his mouth occasionally when he turned his head for air. After more than thirty-five minutes of steady swimming, he shifted to a breaststroke for the last one hundred meters.

Pat kept the boat between himself and the house as he slowly closed on the boat. Once he reached it, he traversed to the stern and peeked around to have a look at the house, checking for any activity from within. He climbed the stern ladder next to the rudder and pulled on the line, retrieving his bag. Once inside the small cabin, he peeled off his wetsuit. He used the towel he'd brought in his cinch bag to dry off, and then put his clothes back on. He closed the cabin door and sat down on the lone bed. In the dark, from feel, he screwed the GM-9 suppressor to his SIG 226 and lay back on the bed with the pistol on his chest, closing his eyes.

He awoke to the sound of oars in the water. It was dark in the cabin, but he was able to see the luminous dial on his watch and determine he had slept for just over four hours. He felt the sailboat shift when the rowboat made contact with the sailboat, and again with the weight of a man climbing onto the deck from the stern ladder. For the next fifteen minutes, he could hear the sails being unfurled, and minutes later he felt the boat go underway. Pat allowed another ten minutes for the sailboat to get some distance from the house, and then he opened the door with his left hand while aiming his pistol with his right. Thomas was seated at the edge of the stern with the rudder in one hand and a line in the other.

"Stay on course, Thomas. Any sudden moves and I'll be forced to shoot," he warned as he looked out from the cabin, which was no more than five feet from Thomas. Staring into the dark enclosure with the sun to his front, Thomas could not recognize Pat.

"What do you want?" said Thomas. He was wearing wraparound sunglasses, a red jacket and jeans. He had long blond hair, sideburns and a small soul patch on his chin. Pat slowly uncoiled from the cramped cabin and sat down in front of Thomas, making sure his head was below the boom in case Thomas tried to be clever.

"I have some questions for you, Thomas," said Pat. With the sunglasses on, Pat couldn't see Thomas's eyes, but the body language made it clear that Thomas recognized him.

"What is it you want to know?" Thomas said in a German accent.

"Who hired you to have me killed?" said Pat.

"Nobody hired me. I have no idea of what you're talking about."

Without a moment's hesitation, Pat pulled the trigger of the pistol in his right hand and shot Thomas in the right knee. Barely uttering a cry, Thomas fell forward and blacked out. With nobody at the controls, the sailboat heaved too. The boom swung at Pat and he ducked to miss it, while the boat tipped and almost capsized.

Still sitting, Pat reached over and grabbed the halyard, releasing the line and dropping the main sail. He jumped up and tied the sails down and then secured the boom. Once the boat was secure, he shifted his attention to Thomas, whose eyes were fluttering and showing signs of regaining consciousness. Pat used a sail tie down to bind Thomas's wrists in front of him. When he moved his leg to bind his ankles, Thomas shrieked with pain. Pat held his ankles together and finished the job before jumping back to his seat.

Seated across from Thomas in the stern of the sailboat, Pat slapped the man's sunglasses off his face.

"You have five more seconds to answer my last question," said Pat in a calm voice.

"My company was hired by a law firm in New York. I don't know the name of the client," said Thomas. The suppressed 9mm made a loud spitting sound when Pat fired the next round into the man's left elbow. Already in shock, Thomas didn't pass out this time. Instead, he howled in a gut-wrenching scream. The scream was so loud, Pat did a visual check to see if anyone was within hearing distance. The boat was adrift, but it was in the center of the lake, at least a mile from either shore, and there were no other watercraft in the area. Thomas was free to scream all he wanted. Blood was pooling on the deck, and Thomas was shaking and moaning.

"Answer the damn question," said Pat.

"They'll kill my family. Please," said Thomas.

"Maybe you're forgetting, but you sent three men to kill me and they almost succeeded. I'm going to ratchet up the pain until you answer the question," Pat said as he raised the pistol and took aim at the man's good knee.

"Barney Bellomo. The man who hired me is the lawyer who represents Barney Bellomo," said Thomas.

"Who's Barney Bellomo?"

"He's a New York Mafia leader."

"Who's the lawyer?" said Pat.

"His name's Anthony Rizzo."

"Give me the details on the contract. When were you hired, and what were the conditions?"

"One hundred and fifty thousand dollars advance. Two hundred thousand when the job was done," Thomas said.

"How did you know I was in Brussels?"

"The lawyer contacted me. He said the target was in Brussels, so I sent a team to Brussels."

"How did they know where to ambush me?"

"Same thing, two days after the team arrived we were given a time and place where you would be by the lawyer," Thomas said.

"How do you contact the lawyer?"

"On the darknet, using Google Messenger."

"How do I find Anthony Rizzo?"

"I've never met him. He sets up weapons buys, and he hires my services," Thomas said.

"How does he pay you?" Pat said.

"Bitcoin."

"Anything else you think I should know before I go after these people?" Pat asked.

"Please, just let me go. I'll forget the contract. I'm sorry. Please, I have a family," said Thomas.

Pat fired one round into the man's temple and a second round into his heart. He grabbed the body by the restraints around his ankles and dragged it into the cabin and shut the door. He took a bailing bucket and doused the deck with lake water until no more blood was visible. He then started the small outboard and returned the boat to its mooring.

Pat disassembled the handgun and tossed it into the water, then used the rowboat to return to his hotel across the lake. Once on shore, he threw his equipment bag over his shoulder and walked back to the Romantik Seehotel and checked out.

He expected the police would eventually retrace his steps, but he had checked in with a fake identity, and he didn't expect the body to be discovered for several hours, if not days. He had already packed the car before starting the mission, so he went straight to the car and headed off to the airport to catch a flight to the United States.

Chapter 16

Arlington, Virginia

Pat instantly regretted refusing the general anesthetic. He was flat on his back in an improvised operating room that, based on the dresser and vanity, had once been a bedroom. His knuckles were beginning to ache from gripping the rails on the hospital bed while he focused his vision on the overhead fan, trying to hypnotize himself with the rotating blades. The doctor had injected three shots of local anesthetic around the hole in his thigh, but it was nowhere near up to the task. He could feel every movement as the doctor probed, cut and occasionally extracted material from the wound. He would occasionally glance down to see what the doctor and nurse were doing, but they had built a plastic dam around the wound and were crouched in so close it was impossible to see. After what felt like an eternity, the doctor finally stopped the body invasion and sutured the wound.

"It's time to roll over, so I can work on the entrance wound," said the doctor.

Sweat was beading on Pat's forehead, and he rolled over to allow the doctor to repeat the process on the back of his thigh. Facedown, he pressed his forehead hard into the bed. He had no way to measure time, but the entrance wound seemed to take a lot less time before the pain eventually ended. Once a bandage was applied, the nurse gently guided him to roll onto his back.

"That wound is going to leave an ugly scar. I found two shell fragments and a small chunk of fabric in that leg of yours. Now it will heal properly. Stay in bed for the next three days. I'm going to leave you on the drip for another twenty-four hours. Nurse Rachele will look after you," said the doctor.

The masked nurse with the pretty eyes slid Pat over to a gurney and wheeled him down a corridor, depositing him onto a queen-sized bed in one of the many empty bedrooms inside the safe house. If caring for a patient who insisted on keeping a pistol at his side during an operation while refusing to accept a general anesthetic was even a bit unusual, she gave no indication. Pat placed his Walther PPQ M2 under his pillow and fell asleep.

He woke when he felt a punch to his shoulder. Instinctively he reached for his pistol.

"Take it easy, Ranger, I'm a friendly," Mike said.

"I hope so," said Pat.

"How do you like the accommodations?"

"Not bad. How long was I out?"

"Six hours, according to the nurse. How do you feel?"

"My leg feels a lot better. I think that spook doctor of yours did the trick," Pat said.

"How long were you walking around with that junkyard in your leg?" Mike asked.

"Almost two weeks. You should already know that," Pat said.

"I do, I just want to see if our stories match."

"If your version of events is coming from official CIA channels, then I'm guessing they won't," said Pat.

"Let me hear your version first. Start from when you arrived in Brussels," Mike said.

Pat spent the next forty-five minutes describing his actions while in Brussels. The only part he left out was the dying breath interrogation of the third gunman.

"How do you think the gunmen knew your location?" said Mike.

"The only person I talked to about the meet was Natalia. Either she tipped them off or she told someone else who did."

"Somebody may have been listening in."

"Unlikely," Pat said.

"Where did you call Natalia from? Is it possible there were listening devices in your room?"

"To bug my room, the bad guys would have had to know where I was staying. If they had that information, then why didn't they finish me off after the attack? Why let me live off room service for a week without making another attempt?"

"I'll buy that, but what about your phone? If you called Natalia, someone could have gotten the number and tracked the cell phone."

"I had five Belgian SIM cards. I tossed the one I used to call Natalia immediately after the call."

"You think it was Natalia?" Mike said.

"I'm not positive, but she's definitely the prime suspect. Four guys in a gunfight, probably fifty unsuppressed rounds fired at me. All from within fifty meters of the rendezvous location. Where was she? What was her reaction?" Pat asked.

"She exfiltrated and returned to base, which is what she's been trained to do."

"Who did she tell about the rendezvous?"

"I don't know. Possibly other members of the JTTF or the head of station in Brussels, or even my counterpart who manages operations in Europe," said Mike.

"I would really like to get an answer to that question. Why don't I go back to Brussels and ask her myself? I'm sure the Botox queen would love to see me again," Pat said.

"I'll go to the director and he'll get the information through channels. There's no benefit to airing our suspicions prematurely."

"Sue-Sue suggested the DNI was involved in this whole conspiracy business. What makes you think we can trust the director?"

"He's career Agency. I've known the man for two decades. He's as solid as they come. He's the one man we can trust. And don't put so much faith in the word of your boom-boom girl. She's Chinese intelligence. She lies for a living," Mike said.

"I almost went to Sue-Sue for help. I wouldn't let the doctor put me out, because the only one I trust right now is you. My greatest fear is that your employer would finish what they started," Pat said.

"Someone within the US intel community is involved in this, I'll grant you that. We knew we had an inside problem when Fouad Zhattari was hit, but it's not productive to lash out at everyone. We need to continue to keep the circle tight while we continue the investigation."

"How tight, Mike? How tight is tight enough. I think from now on we keep things between us and no one else. How about you tell me the names of every person who's going to have access to this conversation? Then, if the risk seems reasonable, I'll tell you the parts I left out," Pat said.

"You left parts out?" Mike said.

"I told you everything that explains where I've been. I left out the parts that point to where I'm going. I'm tired, I'm hurt and I'm on the run. This isn't a good time to fight through another ambush."

"You think I would set you up?"

"No, I don't. I think someone above you or around you will set me up, like the DNI," said Pat.

"In consideration of your current state, with an abundance of caution I will restrict the need to know to two more people.

The deputy director for clandestine operations and the director," said Mike.

"Can you keep the director from sharing with the DNI?"

"I'm fairly sure he'll understand. Plus, none of this is especially flattering to the Agency. What did you hold out from me?" Mike said.

"I was able to persuade one of the attackers to divulge the name of his boss. Thomas Kriss is an arms dealer who owns a guns-for-hire business on the side. His teams are mostly Eastern European former special forces. We're acquaintances. He actually had a pretty good reputation as a trader. I had no idea he'd branched out into the mercenary business. He lives in Zurich. I went to visit him, and he admitted accepting a contract to kill me. He told me the contract was given to him by Anthony Rizzo, an attorney in New York. He said Rizzo represents one of the mob bosses. Some guy named Bellomo," Pat said.

"Where is Kriss now?"

"I'm pretty sure he's still in Zurich."

"Is he alive?"

"No."

"How did he die?" Mike asked.

"Badly, on his one good knee, begging," Pat said.

"We could have learned a lot more if you had brought him in."

"I doubt it. He was very concerned about what the mob would do to him if he talked. It would take a lot more than withholding his daily sitcom at Club Gitmo to make him overcome that kind of fear. The average teenaged kid doing two-a-days to make the high school football team endures more punishment than what those babysitters at Gitmo call interrogation."

"Don't be so sure about that," Mike said.

"Besides, I think I did him a favor. If the mob knows he's dead, they should leave his family alone. What's the point in scaring a dead guy, right?"

"So, you did him a favor."

"Kind of," said Pat.

"What are you thinking about doing next?"

"I'm going to keep rolling up this line of string I found until I get to the source."

"Are you going after Bellomo?"

"First, I want to talk to Rizzo. Then Bellomo and then whoever Bellomo is working for in this sordid mess."

"I can't think of a single reason why any of the New York crime families would be involved in this kind of conspiracy. Loan sharking, drugs, prostitution, the docks, the unions, the trash business, yes. Funding ISIS to alter the global balance of power and influence US foreign policy, definitely not. I would be surprised if any one of them could even point out Syria on a map," Mike said.

"I don't have a clue myself, but I'm pretty sure once I hang this ginzo mobster off a tall building by his ankles, he'll explain it all pretty damn quick," said Pat.

"The top mobsters will have twenty-four-hour surveillance from the feds. Getting to them undetected isn't going to be easy. If they identify you, the feds will arrest you on sight."

"I didn't come to you before I went to Zurich because even physically degraded, that was an easy mission. I came to you this time because I realize I can't do it without your support. I don't know anything about the mob. I need intel on who these people are, where they work, where they live, how they're organized and how they defend themselves. Plus, I need weapons, lots of weapons and gear too."

"You realize the CIA cannot operate domestically," Mike said.

"This is one of those times when I like being the assistant to the regional manager, Michael. I'm not an employee, I'm a rogue contractor. A wanted rogue contractor. I can do whatever I want, I just need a little information and a few misplaced weapons systems," Pat said.

"Let me see what I can do. Get some rest—this may take a few days," said Mike.

Chapter 17

New York City

The office building he was looking for was on the corner of Lexington and Fortieth, less than five minutes from Grand Central Station. It was just after noon on a warm, sunny autumn day. The sidewalk was crowded with pedestrians dressed in business attire. He found his building and slipped into the rotating doors and entered the lobby.

His meeting was at twelve thirty and he had some time to kill. He sat in the lobby and studied the crowd that was trickling out the elevators and flowing through the access points and though the lobby and into the much larger torrent of people on the sidewalk. He couldn't help but be reminded of the documentary movie, *March of the Penguins.*

The lobby was sparsely decorated. It consisted of only a visitor's desk and a handful of art deco chairs scattered about. It was a deliberately nondescript building in a city known for landmark towers. A list of companies was posted above the visitor's desk. None of them were names he recognized except the law firm of Cohen, Sanchez and Pataki. If nothing else, the Jewish, Hispanic and Italian-named partners were a tribute to New York's multiculturalism.

Pat obtained a pass at the security desk. The guard took his driver's license and verified he had an appointment with the receptionist upstairs before allowing him to continue. Cohen, Sanchez and Pataki's offices were upmarket and in line with what Pat expected from a Manhattan law office, with the plush carpets and expensive furnishings that screamed of successful settlements to future clients. David Cohen was the senior partner who had unsuccessfully defended Barney Belem on RICO charges. Although receiving only twelve years may have been a victory of sorts. Anthony Rizzo was the junior partner Pat was scheduled to meet.

On his arrival, the receptionist escorted him into a conference room. Pat had called a few days earlier to schedule an engagement meeting. He'd used one of his aliases, Ron Springfield, and requested a meeting with Anthony Rizzo under the guise that he was interviewing attorneys to handle a business acquisition. The conference room sat twelve, with a huge table made from a single slab of hardwood. The walls were tastefully decorated with landscape prints.

Pat placed his leather briefcase on the floor next to his chair and swiveled toward the doorway. After a few minutes, a man entered the room. He was alone, carrying a yellow legal pad in his left hand. He was slim, six-two, dark-haired with Italian features, a good-looking man. The file Mike had provided Pat on Anthony said he was thirty-four years old, Columbia undergrad and NYU law graduate. Anthony was a native New Yorker, who was gay and had a live-in boyfriend.

Pat stood when Anthony Rizzo entered the room and the two men closed to shake. When Anthony extended his hand, Pat hit him in the jaw with a left cross that knocked him unconscious. At six-five, two hundred and twenty, Pat packed a hammer fist. He grabbed Anthony's suit as the man fell away, preventing a hard fall. He pivoted the younger man and sat him on one of the conference room tables. Pat then walked over to the door and locked it.

He opened his briefcase, pulled out a suppressed pistol and set it aside. He removed the chemical interrogation kit, opened it and removed the first syringe marked with the letter A. Anthony was regaining consciousness when Pat stuck the syringe into his neck. He hit the carotid artery head-on and injected the sodium amatol into his system. Anthony's eyes began to focus. For a second, it looked like Anthony was going to scream until a calm appeared over his face. Pat slapped Anthony in the face.

"Anthony, I want you to have a look at this box. Do you see how many needles I have? Some are marked with an A and some are marked with a B. Can you see that? The one I just gave you has an A on it. The A needles contain sodium amatol, among other things. The A needles will make you relax and help you answer my questions. The syringes marked B are more complicated. I really don't have any idea what's in the drug cocktail—I just know that if I don't tie down your hands, you're going to tear off your face and pull out your eyes to try to stop the burning. The way this works is, I give you needle A to relax and talk, and I give you needle B to punish you if you don't talk. We'll rinse and repeat until you give me what I need. How does that sound?" said Pat.

"Why are you doing this to me?" Anthony said with a slight slur.

"The question is, why did you hire Thomas Kriss to kill Pat Walsh?"

"I don't know what you're talking about."

"Time to test drug B," said Pat as he removed the tie-downs from his briefcase and slowly secured Anthony's flaccid arms to the armchair.

"I did what I was ordered to do," Anthony said, straining against the ties.

"By who?" said Pat.

"By Mr. Bellomo."

"Why did he order the murder?"

"I don't know."

"How did you know where and when to ambush Pat Walsh in Brussels?" said Pat.

"I received a call."

"From who?"

"I don't know. It was from an unknown number, and the man didn't identify himself," said Anthony.

"I don't believe you." Pat plunged a needle marked B into Anthony's neck. Before the drug could kick in, Pat tied a gag around his mouth. After ten minutes, he injected an A needle into Anthony's neck.

"Who gave you the information on Pat Walsh in Brussels?" said Pat.

"It was a blocked number, that's all I know. The person never identified himself."

"How did you know the information was legitimate?"

"I was told I would get a call within a few days by Mr. Bellomo, and I did. That's all I know, I'm just a messenger," Anthony said.

"How do you communicate with Bellomo?"

"I meet with him at his restaurant. He never uses the phone."

The interrogation lasted for twenty-five more minutes and Pat used the B needle two more times. In the end, he felt he had gotten all the details possible on how Bellomo had ordered the hit and how he'd communicated with Kriss. Pat removed the ties from the man's wrists, returned everything to his briefcase and left the room with Anthony conscious, sitting upright but completely unresponsive in his chair.

Once back on the street, he hailed a cab to Mazzaro's restaurant on Forty-Second Street. It was almost 3 p.m., and the lunch crowd had thinned by the time he arrived. Pat requested a table next to the front window. The waitress who returned was a heavyset Dominican woman with a pleasant smile. Pat ordered the chicken parmesan and sparkling water and returned to the task of reconnaissance. Barney Bellomo owned the restaurant. According to the information Mike had extracted from the FBI Organized Crime Task Force, Bellomo's routine was to arrive every day at four to five in the afternoon and leave every evening at nine.

The restaurant had two floors. The kitchen was an open affair located on the first floor, which left room for only ten tables. He imagined that, without a kitchen to get in the way, the second floor had at least twenty tables. The neighborhood was a mixture of retail and residential buildings. The restaurant had valet parking. There were no available parking spaces on the street. He studied the windows of the parked cars, trying to locate the FBI detail, but he couldn't. Given the many years they'd had Bellomo under surveillance, he thought it more likely the FBI would have leased one of the apartments across the street to use as a long-term observation point.

He scanned every window. Because of the angle, it had to be a lower floor—nothing higher than the fourth floor would have an angle into the restaurant. He found a couple of likely spots for the surveillance, but nothing conclusive.

Midway through his huge serving of chicken parmesan, a black Mercedes sedan pulled up to the front door. The valet opened the rear sedan door and Barney Bellomo stepped out. A second man exited the passenger-side door and a third exited the back of the sedan from the door opposite Barney. The mob boss did not fit the gangster stereotype—at least what Pat had come to expect from watching *Sopranos*. Bellomo wore a beige linen suit with a white shirt and no tie. His only jewelry was a watch and a wedding ring. He had a dark complexion and a medium build, with grey hair and a deeply receding hairline. He looked older than his seventy years, with a jowly face and bags under his eyes.

Bellomo was greeted warmly by the staff as he entered the restaurant. The hostess held the door for him and the waiters on the floor all stopped what they were doing to say hello. The stairs to the second floor were next to the hostess station, and Barney immediately began the slow climb upward, trailed by his two-man security detail.

Pat finished his meal and went to the restroom to look for a back exit. If there was one, it was only accessible through the kitchen. He paid the tab and caught a taxi back to his hotel.

At eight thirty, Pat was seated at a table in the Starbucks across the street from Mazzaro's. It was a warm early-fall night. He was wearing a pair of Merrill boots, blue jeans, a leather bomber jacket and a Yankees cap. He was on his second coffee when he spotted the same black Mercedes from the afternoon pull in front of the restaurant.

The traffic was steady and he cautiously jaywalked across the street. One of the security men opened the restaurant door for Bellomo. The valet already had the back door open by the time Pat reached the sidewalk and began to approach the car from the back. Pat was less than ten feet away when the aged Barney began to slide into the backseat. Pat withdrew his suppressed 9mm Walther and shot the lead security guard in the forehead. He pushed Bellomo the rest of the way into the Mercedes. The trailing security man, who had been holding the front door to the restaurant, managed to unholster his pistol before Pat put two bullets into his chest at a range of twenty feet. He elbowed Barney in the head, sending him sprawling across the backseat, and jammed his pistol into the back of the driver's head.

"Drive and keep both hands on the wheel," he said. The driver pulled into the traffic as Pat closed the car door. "Turn right at the light."

Pat withdrew a pen-sized hard case from his jacket pocket and removed a syringe. He plunged the ketamine into Barney, who was still dazed from the vicious elbow to the forehead.

"Turn left at the light," said Pat. The driver still had not said a word. "Pull over and stop here." Once the car came to a halt, Pat ordered, "Put the car in park." He shot the driver in the head and then opened the car door, pulling Bellomo behind him. Once he had him all the way out of the car, he threw the old man over his shoulder. He walked a few steps and, using his free hand, opened the back door of the rented Chevy Tahoe he had positioned earlier on the road. He tossed Barney in the back and jumped into the driver's seat.

Barney did not regain consciousness until eight hours later. When he woke, he was naked and blindfolded, bound to a chair by his hands and feet.

"That noise you hear is the Saco River. This is a small section of white water. It's a little loud, but we can still carry on a conversation. Its loud enough that nobody can hear you scream—not that it matters, because the nearest person is probably more than ten miles away," Pat said.

"You're going to die. Do you know who you're fucking with?" said Barney.

"Yeah, I know who you are, and it really pisses me off to have to waste my skills on lowlife mafia scum. I was trained to deal with warriors. It's embarrassing, I mean it. Me dealing with you is like... it's like, who's a good Yankees pitcher? Chapman. Let's use Chapman. It's like Chapman pitching in a high school ball game. Embarrassing. I hope nobody finds out—my reputation will be shot," Pat said.

"I'm going to peel your skin off, I'm going to flay you, I'm going to kill your family and everyone and everything you ever cared about and make you watch. I'm going to make you wish you never lived. Do you hear me? Do you hear me?" Bellomo yelled.

"Look, I get that you're some sort of mafia Juan or something. I need some answers to some very important questions, and you obviously aren't in the right frame of mind to answer them. I have some things to do. I'll come back when you're in a more cooperative mood. I wish I could show you the scenery. It's beautiful. The most annoying thing about Maine are the blackflies. Those bites—the bugs are so tiny, but the bite is huge. How something that little can cause so much pain—it's unnatural, don't you think?

"Second worst are the mosquitos. I've heard people call them the state bird. Honestly, they can make you crazy. They swarm and they just won't leave you alone. They fly into your ears and into your nose and eyes, and that buzzing won't go away. In some ways, they're like those damn fire ants that are all over the place, like the ones who made a nest in that log next to you. I just hate them. Anyway, enjoy the fresh air. I'll be back," Pat said.

Pat got up and walked away from Bellomo. Before he left, he checked the McQ device to ensure the thermal and day optic video stream was working. The video data stream was sent via radio link to his laptop. Although there were other cabins nearby, it was offseason, and Pat was sure he and Bellomo were the only people for miles.

The cabin was a well-furnished two-bedroom log structure with a nice view of the river. There was power, but no television or Wi-Fi. He did have a cell phone signal, which was good. After a six-hour sleep he woke up and grilled a steak for dinner. The temperature was down to fifty-eight degrees, which was uncomfortable for Barney, but survivable. The cold would kill the mosquitos in another month, but at the moment they were as big and bad as ever.

Periodically, he would check the video stream to see how Bellomo was doing. Barney was in some distress. He was jerking his head in different directions and flapping his elbows as best he could. Being eaten by blackflies all day and mosquitos all night was a brutal experience, especially for a city dweller unaccustomed to the wilderness. At the moment, he had a cloud of gnats around his head and was shaking his head, trying to keep them away.

At 4 p.m. the next day, Pat returned to Barney and removed his blind fold.

"Kill me, just fucking kill me," said Barney in a dry rasp.

"I'll help you out, but only after you answer my questions," said Pat.

"Okay," said Barney.

Barney was covered in welts from insect bites. His eyes were bloodshot and wild, he had tears flowing down his cheeks, and he was sobbing.

"Please stop this. Please, I'm begging you," Barney said.

"Why did you order the hit on Pat Walsh?" Pat asked.

"Mike Genovese requested it."

"Who's Mike Genovese?"

"He's the Chairman and CEO of G3."

"What do you have to do with G3?"

"Mike's old man used to be the boss. He died in prison. When Mike started his business after college, I invested out of respect for his father. Mike is a good businessman and he built a big company. When Mike has a problem that cannot be handled through normal business channels, he asks me for help, and if it makes sense I help," Barney said.

The interrogation lasted sixteen hours. Pat recorded it all. When it was over, he had all the details on how Michael Genovese was able to win defense contracts by sabotaging and stealing from the competition. Barney had also explained the methods used to buy several key government officials, including two senators and five congressmen who were members of the Armed Forces Committees. Pat found the story about how Lucian Rossi's electoral victory had been secured by overdosing the seventeen-year-old daughter of his opponent particularly upsetting.

What Barney Bellomo had not been able to reveal was why Michael Genovese had ordered his execution. His only explanation was that Pat Walsh was a threat to the business.

Once Pat felt he had everything Bellomo knew about Michael Genovese's operation, he stopped the interrogation. He looked at the man seated across from him and saw a frail, broken old man. He walked over to the tripod and shut off the video camera. He was on day two of the interrogation, and Barney clearly had no more information to give. He was physically and emotionally spent. The insects no longer seemed to bother him. His voice was a raspy whisper and he was barely coherent.

Pat withdrew his pistol from the shoulder holster and screwed on the can. He raised the weapon, and Barney raised his head, made eye contact and growled like a dog. Pat carefully aimed and squeezed off two rounds, one in the head and then one in the heart. He retrieved the two spent shell casings and walked away.

Chapter 18

New York City

Nicky Terranova was escorted to Michael's theater room by Daphne, his latest mail-order companion. The leering behavior and clever quips from Nicky about his latest hottie were absent this day. Nicky was obviously distracted. The two men rotated the theater recliner chairs so they were facing each other. It was seven at night and Michael and Daphne were both dressed for dinner. Daphne was a tall Indonesian girl. She was lithe and pretty, with long black hair, brown eyes and a sweet smile that never shut off. She was clearly fond of playing the lady of the manor. It was Daphne's second day off the airplane, and her fantasy trip to New York City with a handsome young billionaire was everything she had dreamed it would be—so far, at least.

Once Daphne left the room, Nicky hopped up from his seat and locked the door.

"What's so urgent that it couldn't wait?" Michael said.

"They found Barney. His body was dumped in a landfill in Bangor, Maine," said Nicky.

"He had a lot of enemies. Who got to him?"

"This is on you, Michael. You made a serious mistake. Now I'm going to be next."

Michael got up from his chair and poured a double scotch from the decanter, handing it to Nicky. "You need to calm yourself before you say something you can't take back. What do you mean this is on me?"

"Everything has backfired. The hit team that went after Pat Walsh is dead. They ambushed him on his way to a meet. We were tipped and they caught him by surprise. All three were killed during the attack, and Walsh escaped. These guys were pros, Michael. They caught him completely by surprise, and the only person who walked away was Walsh.

"Two weeks later, the guy we hired to do the hit, Thomas Kriss, is found dead on his sailboat in Zurich. Kriss was tortured. Walsh shot him up bad. He got everything he wanted out of him, and then he killed him. When word got out that Barney went missing last week, Anthony Rizzo came forward.

"Pat Walsh met Rizzo in his office. Made an appointment and then sauntered right in like it was a regular meeting. He tortured Anthony inside his own law office, during work hours, with the entire company outside the door. He used some sort of chemical. People from the office found him in a catatonic state, just sitting in the meeting room drooling. He spent the next week in the hospital under psychiatric observation.

"When he was released, he learned Barney went missing and he came forward. The security tapes from Rizzo's office prove it was Pat Walsh that visited him. Same day Walsh visits Rizzo, Barney goes missing. He kills the security detail and hijacks Barneys car, with him in it. Kriss, Rizzo and Barney were all tortured. Kriss gave up Rizzo. Rizzo gave up Barney. Who do you think Barney gave up? We're next, you and me," Nicky said.

"Have you talked to Rizzo? How much did he tell Walsh?" Michael asked.

"Rizzo has been disappeared. His days of talking are over. He was Barney's messenger. Every direction Barney gave was through him. He knew a lot—he knew too much. Same with Barney. He also knew everything, and Walsh must have wrung everything out of him. He had Barney for days," Nicky said.

"Barney knew very little about my operation," Michael said.

"He knew enough to put both of us in prison for the rest of our days."

"The government doesn't capture and torture US citizens, and we have some very good protection inside the government. No need to worry about the law."

"Walsh is coming for us," Nicky said.

"Yeah, on that point I agree. When was Barney killed?"

"Six days ago, plus or minus a day, according to the police."

"That's a lot of time. If Walsh is after us, why hasn't he made his move?" Michael said.

"Going after Walsh was a huge mistake. We need to find a way to make peace with this man. He wasn't a threat to begin with. You should have left him alone. There was no cause to set him up for the Brussels bombing. That was incredibly stupid."

Michael sprung up from his chair and punched the much older man with a straight right in the face, while he was still sitting. Nicky and the recliner both fell completely back, leaving Nicky dazed and staring at the ceiling. Nicky's nose and mouth were bleeding, and he was spitting out teeth.

"I told you to watch what you say," Michael said. Nicky rolled out of the chair and sat on the floor on his hands and knees, looking up at Michael.

"If you think I'm afraid of you, you're out of your fucking mind. I'm a made man. Do you have any idea what that fucking means? I don't think you'll survive Walsh, but if you do, you're still going to have to deal with the family over what you just did. You're a dead man, Michael. Dead," Nicky said through broken teeth and a badly bleeding mouth.

"The family was living off peanuts until I showed you how to make real money. After the Chin was hoisted to prison, Barney stepped up, but he was so afraid of following the Chin to jail, he barricaded himself behind layers and layers and lived like a princess in a tower. Protection rackets, the unions, the docks—the revenues were all dropping. The family isn't going to do a damn thing. I saved you people from extinction. I make you millions—legitimate, clean, laundered millions—hundreds of millions every year. If I send word you've lost your nerve, the next guy to disappear isn't going to be me, it'll be you," Michael said.

Nicky went to the bathroom and returned with a damp towel, which he pressed to his damaged face. "We need to find a way out of this. Make Walsh an offer, as you say. He's not government. He can be bought," he said.

"I don't think he can be bought. He already has money. I think he's a crusader. The only way to stop Walsh is going to be to kill him," Michael said.

"How are we going to do that?"

"Like you said, he's coming after us. We need to set a trap."

"We need to increase our security until we have a plan."

"You should stay here. I'll bring in some professionals to protect us. We'll turn this place into a fortress. This is the thirty-fourth floor. The only entrances are the elevator and the stairs. Easy to secure, easy to guard," Michael said.

"I can't stay. I gotta meet with some people later. You created this problem. Now you need to fix it. That's the message from the family. Either clean up your mess or you're finished," Nicky said.

"Understood," said Michael.

Chapter 19

Arlington, Virginia

Mike Guthrie had been at the safe house with Pat since the early morning. He and Pat watched the videos of the interrogation of Bellomo in their entirety.

"Is this the only copy?" said Mike.

"No, I have one more," said Pat.

"Keep that second copy safe. I'm going to take this one to the director."

"What'll he do with the information?"

"The tape proves that Michael Genovese has at least one committee senator and four congressmen in his pocket. Bellomo only knew the ones his organization got to. He refers to others who are involved. The information has to go to the attorney general. How it gets there and in what form is going to be up to the director," Mike said.

"What do you mean, in what form?" Pat said.

"I'm no lawyer, but these tapes are going to be a problem for law enforcement. The only crime they really show is that you're a murderer. The director would never hand them over to the attorney general in their entirety. This isn't the Agency's lane to begin with. He'll have to be careful how he hands this info over to the Feds."

"The tapes show how the mafia got control of key members of the Congressional Armed Services and Intelligence Committees through bribery, blackmail and election rigging. At least, I think extorting your political opponents and forcing them to withdraw is a form of election rigging. That is all national security stuff—how can that not be in the CIA's lane?" Pat said.

"It is and it isn't. Director Pasternak is a good man. He knows his way around Washington. He'll get the information actioned by the right people."

"I hope so. According to the Chinese, his boss the DNI is in on it."

"That isn't what the Chinese said. They said the DNI knew about Fouad Zhattari. That doesn't mean he was in on it."

"If it walks like a duck," Pat said.

"What about Mike Genovese?" Mike asked.

"By now, he knows what happened to Anthony Rizzo and Barney Bellomo. I'm sure he thinks he's next."

"Is he?"

"No."

"I think you've done enough. You should go back to the Bahamas and let the appropriate law enforcement agencies handle this," Mike said.

"I have no confidence in the US government's ability to deal with this corruption. All the bad guys are winning in this deal. The unelected deep state guys are controlling our foreign policy, the defense companies are making huge profits, and the dirty politicians are winning elections. Even those who aren't winning have more of an incentive to keep it quiet than to blow it up. It's a huge scandal that'll damage the administration even if they aren't involved. Once you give that tape to your boss, you need to worry about your own safety, because those

Washington swamp creatures are going into coverup mode," Pat said.

"I don't think that'll be the case," Mike said.

"Somebody at the top of the intel food chain set me up in Brussels. That is an undeniable fact. When you turn in those tapes to the CIA director, it seems likely that the same person who tipped Thomas Kriss to ambush me will target both of us."

"The director is the one who went to bat for you and cleared you when you were set up for the Brussels thing. He's one of the good guys."

"I'm sure he is, but somebody above him or below him is trying to have me killed."

"Do you think it would be better if we held onto these tapes for a while?"

"No, I think you have to give them to the director. But I think once you do, they'll go into coverup mode. If Michael Genovese is at the top of this thing, he'll start cleaning house, eliminating the people who know too much. If he isn't the one calling the shots, then I bet he'll be the first one taken out in the cleanup effort," Pat said.

"What's your plan?" Mike asked.

"I'm going back to New York. I'm going to have a talk with Terranova. You turn in the tapes to your ring-knocker buddy Pasternak. I think once Terranova is dead, the wise guys will be effectively out of the picture, leaving only two groups: the corporate players and the politicos. Once the tapes hit, I think we'll learn a lot by who makes the first move," Pat said.

"What do you mean?"

"If you can keep track of who sees the tapes and gets the information, we can learn a lot by how they clean this up. We might be able to find out who's calling the shots, and what they do first should show us where they think they're most exposed. After we found who diverted the claymores, they moved quick to cancel Fouad Zhattari, but that was early stage, and we didn't have any system in place to find out who gave the order and who tipped the bad guys. This time, we need to prepare in advance," Pat said.

"I can keep track of the interrogation tapes. I'll have one of the tech guys plant a tracker that'll send me a message telling me every time the file is opened and by who. The first time it'll be opened will be me showing it to the director. That'll be in a SCIF, and it'll be air gapped to the internet. We'll only be able to trace the movement of the file when it hits systems connected to the web," Mike said.

"That might be able to tell us something," Pat said.

"It's late. I'm going to crash here tonight. Tomorrow, I'll brief the director. You should remain here until he makes a decision. Terranova can wait," Mike said.

Chapter 20

Langley, Virginia

Mike Guthrie spent the morning in his office, working on his presentation to Deputy Director Dave Forrester and Director Bill Pasternak. Dave Forrester managed all clandestine operations for the Agency. When Mike had called and asked for a meeting with the boss, Dave had been quick to get him on the calendar for later in the afternoon. He had Terry O'Reilly, his tech guy, working on putting all the tapes on a single file, with a thirty-minute montage of the most relevant material as the lead-in.

Mike was at his desk when O'Reilly walked into the office and delivered the file on an external hard drive only a few minutes before Mike had to go upstairs for the meeting.

"It's all done, sir," O'Reilly said as he placed the drive on his desk.

"How does the trace work?" Mike asked.

"Every time the file is opened, the time, location and IP address will be sent to us," O'Reilly said.

"If the trace program gets detected, will it be possible to know who the info is being sent to?"

"The route is very complex, and the destination is an anonymous darknet site. Nobody in this building could find out who's receiving the tracking information. I doubt anyone could."

"I need the login instructions, so I can keep up with where this thing goes," Mike said.

O'Reilly handed him the handwritten login instructions on a sheet of paper and left the room.

The meeting was to be held in the small conference room down the hall from the director's office. It was a standard SCIF facility with controlled access, a built-in Faraday cage and electronic equipment approved to hold classified materials. Mike arrived at the director's conference room early to set up for the meeting. He plugged the hard drive into the conference room computer and made sure the video streamed to the large-screen TV on the small round conference table, opposite the chair used by the director. His boss, Dave Forrester, the head of clandestine operations, walked into the conference room as Mike was finishing up his prep.

"The director is going to be few minutes late," Dave said.

"Thanks for setting this up on such short notice," Mike said.

"The boss has a lot going on today. He isn't going to be happy to see this, if it's half as explosive as you mentioned."

"Nobody is going to want to see this video. It's basically a soft coup d'état," Mike said.

"That's just freaking great."

Director Pasternak entered the room like a cyclone. He was a man known for his manic work habits and laser-sharp mind. His background within the Agency was in strategy and analysis, not operations. He had his customary disheveled appearance, with his moppy grey hair askew, his tie loose and his collar open. Looking over his wire-rim reading glasses, he said not a word in greeting. Instead, he nodded to Mike to begin.

"Sir, I know you're on a tight schedule, so I won't repeat any of the background you've been given previously regarding Pat Walsh and the Brussels bombing. I'll restrict this briefing to only new information. It should take less than forty-five minutes," said Mike.

"Go," said the director.

"Pat Walsh was sent to Brussels to identify and locate the mystery woman we have on tape meeting with Ahmed Eleiwi at the Hard Rock Café. On his way to a meeting with our representative on the JTTF who was working the investigation, a Miss Natalia De'Lavega, he was ambushed by three Serbian ex-special forces operators. Although he was wounded in the attack, Walsh killed two of the attackers and was able to briefly interrogate the third before he too died of his wounds. Following the information from the third attacker, Walsh went to Zurich, where he captured, interrogated and killed Thomas Kriss. Kriss confessed to directing the hit on Walsh in Brussels and gave up the name of Anthony Rizzo, a lawyer in New York, as the person who hired him. Walsh went to NYC and conducted an interrogation of Anthony Rizzo. Rizzo confessed to being Barney Bellomo's messenger. Bellomo was the head of the Genovese crime family. He told Walsh that Bellomo ordered the hit. Walsh then went ahead and captured, interrogated and killed Bellomo. This is what Bellomo had to say." Mike clicked the mouse to start the video.

An image of Barney Bellomo tied to a chair, surrounded by trees, filled the screen. The thirty-minute lead-in contained all the key elements of Bellomo's forced confession. It identified Michael Genovese and G3 Technologies as the beneficiaries of actions taken by Bellomo to kill Walsh. It described how the mafia's strong-arm tactics had been used to enable Lucian Rossi to retain his senate seat and how similar tactics had been used to pocket several other members of congress with key committee positions in either Armed Services or Intelligence.

Mike, having viewed the video several times already, concentrated on studying the audience. The director frequently visited Capitol Hill and testified in front of the names mentioned, but he showed little emotion as he viewed the material. David Forrest's temples were pulsing and his hands, on top of the table, were clenched so tight his fingers were white.

"Sir, I have more than thirteen hours of recorded interrogation of Bellomo on this drive. What you have seen are the most salient points. Subject to your questions, this concludes my briefing," Mike said.

"Where's Walsh now?" the director asked.

"He's in one of our safe houses in Arlington."

"You need to keep a leash on that man. We cannot have someone connected to the Agency murdering wise guys in New York. Especially those who are under FBI surveillance."

"Will do."

"What's your take on all of this?" the director asked Mike.

"Major elements of the congressional oversight of our national security structure have been compromised by Michael Genovese for material reasons. The NYC mob participated as a tool to facilitate that compromise. In addition to congress, industry, and the mob, we also have elements within the Agency who are compromised. Someone inside the Agency tipped Genovese, making it possible for him to kill Fouad Zhattari and suppress evidence. Sensitive information regarding the details of the meeting between Natalia and Walsh was also leaked, enabling Genovese to ambush Walsh in Brussels," said Mike.

"Agreed. The motivations of the congressmen involved were explained by Bellomo. The mob's motivation is simple greed, which is also understandable. But why would someone within the Agency or in the executive branch leak sensitive information to Michael Genovese?" said the director.

"Either they're simpatico with Genovese's goals, or he has them in his pocket through blackmail or extortion," said Mike.

"What are Genovese's goals?" said the director.

"Power and greed."

"I don't know anyone in this building who would sign up to make Michael Genovese any richer and more powerful. Which leaves us with the question of how the illiterates in the Italian mafia accomplished what state-sponsored intelligence agencies have failed to do for decades," the director said.

"It's difficult to accept, but the facts speak for themselves."

"How many copies of that video exist?"

"Just the one," Mike said.

"Walsh didn't make a copy?"

"Not that he admits to."

"Anything else I should know?" said the director.

"No."

"Leave the drive."

Mike and Dave got up from the small conference room table and left the room. The director remained at the end of the table, as expressionless as when he had entered.

Mike and Dave did not speak until they were alone in Dave's office, in the sitting area across from Dave's desk.

"What do you think the director is going to do?" Mike said.

"He has no choice but to go directly to the president," Dave said.

"He has to be careful with that video. The CIA executing mobsters in New York is a scandal of almost equal size to some people."

"The director won't suppress that video to protect the Agency. He has to report it. Tell Walsh to lay low for a while before he becomes a liability. His rampage is over. This problem needs to be solved by the big boys," Dave said.

"I'll take care of it," Mike said.

Chapter 21

Brooklyn, New York

Nick Terranova's wife of thirty-four years was serving him lunch in the kitchen. He ate most of his meals at home since being diagnosed with hypertension five years earlier. His wife kept him on a very strict diet. Today's lunch was a vegetarian lasagna, a dish that only someone with his wife's culinary skill could make into something worth looking forward to. The house was small, and the décor dated back to the 1980s. The home had once belonged to his parents.

Nicky was at the table reading the paper while his wife was working at the stove when the doorbell rang. "I'll get it," he said as he stood up from the table.

His wife heard the doorbell ring again and then the sound of Nicky turning the lock. Two deafening blasts were the next sounds she heard before the thud of her husband hitting the floor. She dropped the glass pan holding the lasagna and ran to the front door. Nicky was on his back, holding his chest, and the blood was streaming through his open fingers.

"Michael," was the last word he said.

The first call Nicky's wife made was to 911, although she knew it was already too late. The second call was to Michael. "They killed him," she said.

"Who killed him?"

"I don't know. I was feeding him lunch. Someone came to the door. When he opened the door, they shot him," she said.

"Don't go anywhere. I'll be there as fast as I can," Michael said.

"No, don't come to me. Find them and kill them. They took my Nicky. Promise me you'll find them."

"I promise," he said, and she ended the call.

Michael was at the G3 headquarters. He called both of his brothers and had them meet him in the conference room. When Gino and Louis entered the room, Michael was already seated at the head of the conference table. The two brothers sat next to him.

"Nicky Terranova was killed a few minutes ago," said Michael.

"What happened?" asked Louis.

"He was shot. Annette called a few minutes ago. He opened the door to his house and someone gunned him down. Barney Bellomo was killed last week."

"What's going on?" Gino said.

"I'm not a hundred percent sure, but the family is imploding and we need to take advantage of this opportunity. Nicky was the CEO of GBC Investment, and they hold forty percent of our stock. A while back, I had some people do the research. Nicky was the sole owner of GBC. Barney was always very careful to keep his fingerprints off things. The only guys who would have known about the shareholding would have been Barney, Nicky, and Barney's lawyer, Anthony Rizzo. All of them are out of the picture," said Michael.

"What do you want us to do?" said Gino.

"I want you to buy our stock back," Michael said.

"We don't have that kind of cash. You're talking about more than sixty billion dollars," Gino said.

"Annette is now the owner and signature authority of GBC Investments. I'll go to her and have her sign the purchase agreement. Prepare a transfer of one hundred and fifty-eight million dollars to GBC, and stand by for my instructions on when to execute it," Michael said.

"Why one hundred and fifty-eight million?" said Louis.

"They staked us three different times. The first time was twenty-eight million, then fifty, and the third time one hundred and ten million. Combined, they infused one hundred and fifty-eight million, and in return they received one point two billion in dividends. Now we're going to pay them back and cut our ties. They can no longer do anything for us. In fact, they're a liability and we need to sever our relationship," said Michael.

"If the company buys back this stock, this'll be a huge windfall to the other shareholders," said Louis.

"It's not a buy-back. It'll be a sale of GBC's G3 shares to our holding company. We'll borrow the money from G3 to make the buy and use the annual dividends to pay G3 back before the next audit. With this buy, we'll only have sixteen percent of G3 held outside of the three of us. We'll get that sixteen percent back in due time.

"Gino, get the papers drawn up, and plan to visit Annette after I talk with her. She trusts you. Make sure she knows to leave the money in the account. Make sure she understands that eventually, somebody from the family will come to collect it. Make a transfer of another five million to her personal account to make sure she's okay now that Nicky is gone," Michael said.

Chapter 22

Alexandria, Virginia

It was a crisp fall morning as Lucian Rossi wheeled his Land Rover into the valet stand at the Belhaven Country Club. The autumn foliage was peaking. There was not a cloud in the sky, and the temperature was a comfortable sixty-seven with a gentle, barely noticeable wind. Lucian had a full day planned. It was going to be the ideal Sunday. Eighteen holes, following by brunch at the club and then on to the Redskins game, where he had Owner's Club Suite tickets for the matchup against the Patriots. Lucian could hardly suppress a smile as he passed the doorman at the huge stone entryway on his path into the clubhouse.

Inside the locker room, he met the three other members of this morning's foursome. General Dynamics Electric Boat and the Groton Submarine Base were both very important to the economy of his home state. The contingent today included the two top executives from GDEB and Richard Silver from their lobbying firm, TSG. Lucian had been thrilled earlier in the week to receive the invitation to play golf and attend the football game. He always enjoyed the company of his former senate colleague.

At the ninth hole, Lucian began to experience minor dizziness. After sinking his putt, he asked to be dropped off at the nearby clubhouse and told the other three to play the back nine without him.

"Lucian, are you sure you're going to be okay?" Richard Silver asked as he dropped him at the clubhouse with the golf cart.

"I think I might be catching something. Enjoy the rest of the round. I'll rest up and join with you later at the game," Lucian said.

Alone, inside the locker room, Lucian was sitting on the bench across from his locker, removing his golf shoes, when his vision began to blur. He could feel his hear racing like a freight train, and he felt lightheaded. Holding on to the open locker door, he stood unsteadily to find an attendant when the chest pain struck. A piercing sensation in his heart brought him to his knees in agony. The pain was sudden and fierce. He tried to yell out for help, but his body wouldn't respond. Instead he fell forward. Less than a minute later, he was facedown on the cold tile of the clubhouse floor, dead.

Chapter 23

Eleuthera, Bahamas

It was the height of hurricane season, and Pat was standing at the rail on the second-floor porch of his home near Governor's Harbour, holding a travel mug of coffee and staring into the dark blue Atlantic. Storm surge brought the waterline to within one hundred meters of the house. The crashing of the surf and the roar of the gusting wind drowned out any other noise. Clouds blanketed the sky and the air was moist.

"What do you think?" Pat said.

"Way too messy, looks like a washing machine," Diane said as she surveyed the frothy surf through the bent palm trees obstructing the view to the beach.

"In a few hours, the storm winds will shift to offshore. We're almost in the eye. That's why the rain has stopped."

"Twenty-foot waves—do you think you're up to it?"

"Definitely. Besides, I have a personal lifeguard."

"Yeah, you do," Diane said as she put her arm around his waist and moved her hip to his. Pat took her hand and led her through the sliding glass doors into the master bedroom.

"The surf gods require tribute," he said.

"What does that mean?"

"No idea. I thought it was a clever way to get you back into bed."

"Since when does that require cleverness?" Diane smiled as he led her by the hand to the bed.

Pat let his body go limp as he was spun inside the darkness. The buoyancy of the wetsuit would eventually float him to the surface. The key was not to panic in the disorientation. He could hold his breath for two minutes, and the longest the surf had kept him under today was barely over a minute. Finally, he found the light and broke through to the surface, filling his lungs with air. He quickly pulled the leash at his ankle and brought his board under him. He dodged the sudden impact of an incoming wave by duck-diving below it. Once he surfaced, he used his powerful shoulders and arms to paddle through the impact zone of the breaking waves.

He spotted Diane sitting on her board. A tight red sleeveless wetsuit highlighted the voluptuous contours of her athletic body. Her long dark hair was in a ponytail, silhouetting a classically beautiful face that was surveying the incoming swells. Despite catching the wave after him, she had once again beaten him to the lineup. Diane was often encouraged by her surfing friends to go on the professional tour—she was that good, and Pat never tired of watching her in action. Seeing her dance gracefully on the waves was like poetry, especially when compared to the brutish kamikaze techniques he employed.

"Last run," Pat said. Diane smiled in agreement, knowing her big man was beginning to fatigue.

Pat looked to Diane for the signal to go. She had a lot more experience reading the incoming swells. On her signal, he paddled furiously with strong, hard strokes. His nine-foot big wave board was fast and heavy. When he felt the drop, he popped up into a crouch with his left foot forward and his left hand touching the rail near his ankle. He neared the base on his line and faded to the left, pulling into the pit of the roaring wave. The wave was breaking to the left, and he was in the most powerful part of the barrel.

He raised his left hand to touch the wall of water curling up over him. As the closing barrel enveloped him, he could feel the spray on his neck from the overpressure. Sensing the collapse of the ceiling of water flowing over him, he banked to the right and was knocked off his board by a wall of charging water. Underwater for only a few seconds, he rose to the surface and pulled his board to him by yanking the leash. He rolled onto the surfboard and paddled toward the beach, helped by the surf.

It was his best ride of the day, and he was elated. Exhausted, he staggered to the shoreline in time to see Diane racing inside the barrel of a similar wave. She was graceful and smooth as she ducked out of the barrel seconds before it would have crashed down on her. Within minutes, she and Pat were walking back to the house with boards under their arms.

When they reached the main house, they showered outside. Wrapping themselves in big beach towels, they walked up the stairs to the second-floor deck, where they found Mike Guthrie sitting in a lounge chair. On the table next to him was a pair of binoculars and a tea service. After the greetings, Diane excused herself to shower. Maria, the Filipina who managed the house for Pat, came by and he asked her for two beers.

"You must have a death wish. I can't believe anyone could be crazy enough to surf in these conditions," said Mike.

"I have Diane to rescue me," Pat said.

"She must not know about Sue-Sue, then."

"She does."

"Are you kidding?" said Mike.

"She understands that as an international man of mystery, I sometimes have to sacrifice my body to preserve world peace. It's no big deal."

"Now I know you're lying."

"I am. Diane isn't the jealous type. She's really hot, and she's been watching men behave like fools forever. Anyway, she forgave me."

"So, you benefited from low expectations?" Mike said.

"Yup, that's pretty much my greatest asset."

"What about Sue-Sue?"

"The woman is a professional seductress," Pat said. "The Chinese have a billion people, and she's the one they selected, trained and sent out as a spy into the world to convert patriots into traitors with her feminine charms. What chance did I have? I'm a victim. I should be awarded the CIA's version of the Purple Heart."

"Do you want to be caught up on our case?" said Mike.

"Only if the update includes photos of Michael Genovese strung up by his neck."

"Nicky Terranova is dead. He was executed at his home. Two 9mm rounds to the heart. Lucian Rossi is also dead. He died of a heart attack on a golf course."

"You briefed the CIA director, and two of the biggest loose ends die within the week," Pat said, raising his eyebrows.

"We still have Michael Genovese, Senator Fullman and a handful of congressmen."

"Except for Michael, who I'm guessing is one of the ringleaders, those other guys should hire food tasters."

"I came here with my wife. The person needing protection is me," Mike said.

"Where is she?"

"At a hotel, nearby."

"Go get her. She'll be much safer here. I have Bob McCalister from Kinross working security. He has a nine-man detail providing protection 24/7. His guys have skills."

"I was hoping you would say that, I'll be back in a few," said Mike.

Later, the two men were in the sitting area of Pat's office overlooking the Caribbean Sea. The novelty of being able to see the Atlantic Ocean from his front windows and the Caribbean from the back never grew old for Pat.

"This is a really amazing place. No wonder you don't want to go back to Abu Dhabi," Mike said.

"Your wife will love it here. Maria and Jonah do a great job looking after the place. They live in the guesthouse on the other side of the pool. Father Tellez will be around later. He's another person your wife will want to get to know. He lives in the guesthouse with the chapel attached."

"I never knew you were so religious."

"Father Tellez was our battalion chaplain when I was a company commander during Desert Storm. He's an amazing guy. He retired as a pastor in Miami around the same time I was looking for someone to run the Trident Foundation. He spends about ten minutes a day giving away foundation money and the rest of the time running around tending his flock as the island priest. He's a fascinating guy and a very good friend," Pat said.

"I'm a Methodist, but a priest might be just what we need in this situation," Mike said.

"I was wondering when you were going to get to that."

"We both knew something was wrong when your meet with Natalia turned into an ambush. Anthony Rossi, Barney Bellomo and Thomas Kriss all confirmed the details of the meeting were leaked. We know the info chain backwards ended with the hitters, coming from Kriss, which came from Rossi, which came most likely from Michael Genovese. We don't know who gave the intel to Genovese, and we don't know everyone within the CIA who had the info except for Natalia De'Lavega and her boss. It stands to reason that David Forester, the DDCO, had the info, and the director and possibly the DNI had access, but I don't know that for sure," Mike said.

"Okay, I'm following you."

"When I briefed the director on the Bellomo interrogation, the only other person present was David Forrester. The video was on a single external hard drive. My tech guy put a tracker on the external hard drive that tags every time the file is opened. When access is made to the internet, the tracker program sends the time, location and IP address to an anonymous email address I have," Mike said.

"Have you figured out who's playing for the other team?"

"It's not the Director of National Intelligence who your lady friend alluded to."

"How do you know?" Pat said.

"I briefed the director on Monday at 4 p.m. Nicky Terranova was killed at noon on Tuesday. The video file was opened on Wednesday. It was opened at the director's home on an unsecured computer that was connected to the internet. The program showed the file had only been opened one other time, and that was when I gave the briefing in the director's conference room. On Sunday, Lucian Rossi was killed. Although the cause of death is still a bit of a mystery, I'm confident he was assassinated," Mike said.

"How do we know it isn't David Forrester who's the leak?"

"I don't know for sure, but it's the director who isn't acting straight. After I gave it to him, I expected him to show it to the DNI and then possibly the president. Why take something like that home? I gave that briefing in a SCIF. That video should never touch an unclassified machine."

"They have Terranova and they have Rossi. Whatever they had on the other congressmen was enough to make them traitors, and it should be enough to keep them silent. It would draw too much attention to kill another senator and five members of the House of Representatives. The only step left to fully contain this thing is to silence you."

"These guys seem to favor getting to people through their family. My son is deployed to Afghanistan, so he's out of reach. I was worried about my wife, which is why I took her here," said Mike.

"Nothing short of a full-scale invasion is going to penetrate this compound," Pat said.

"I plan to talk with the DNI. I'm going to need the copy you made of the interrogation file. Without Bellomo's confession and without the tracking data on the hard drive, he's going to have a hard time believing this conspiracy exists and that the director is mixed up in it."

"I should go have a talk with Michael Genovese. A little quality time with him and I'm pretty sure we'll learn all we need to roll this thing up," Pat said.

"Let me talk with the DNI first. Genovese must know you'll be coming for him. He has a lot of resources. Taking him down will require a serious battle, and I promised David Forrest you would be laying low for a while."

"I already have the plan to snatch Genovese. I just need the green light."

"I'm going to fly back to Virginia tomorrow. Hang tight and try not to kill yourself in the surf. I'll let you know once I get some guidance from the White House," Mike said.

"If you're going to be around tonight, we should walk over to Tippy's for dinner," Pat said.

The two couples walked over to Tippy's at last light. There was a slight drizzle, and the pounding surf from the storm was very loud in the background. Eleuthera was a narrow mile-wide strip of land fifty miles west of Nassau, famous for its sandy pink beaches. The most notable restaurant on the island was a mostly open-air affair located directly on the beach. The hidden gem had become instantly famous when it was featured in the

New York Times Sunday section a few years back. Pat loved the authentic beach bum feel to the place. He'd met his surfer girlfriend Diane when she was working at Tippy's as a waitress and he was still building his dream beach house.

Michael's wife, Claire, was a well-maintained woman of fifty-three years. She was an Army brat, who like Mike called Texas home. The two had been married for thirty-one years. They had one son, Michael Junior, who like his dad and his grandfather had graduated from West Point and entered the Army as an infantry lieutenant. Michael Junior was currently serving in Afghanistan with the First Ranger Battalion.

The four took a table in the main restaurant area, overlooking the ocean but protected from the elements. A band was setting up on a small stage area. The four started with mojitos and conch soup.

Pat was wearing a white short-sleeved polo shirt. While the four were making small talk and eating, he noticed Claire repeatedly glancing at his arms. Across both biceps, he had scars that were so old they were practically shadows. The scars were lines across his arms that were so slight most people did not even notice them. Pat picked up on Claire's interest.

"Did Mike tell you how I got these?" Pat said.

Claire nodded.

"The key is the preacher curl," Pat said. The joke failed.

"You have so many scars, I hardly notice anymore. Tell us the story of how you got those," Diane said. Pat looked at Mike for help.

"I'll tell it," Mike said.

"Claire, you met Pat many years ago, when we were dating and he and I were in the Second Ranger Battalion together. Most of the wives and girlfriends stayed clear of Pat and the rest of dedicated bachelors we used to call the he-man woman-haters club. We both did a JSOC assignment in Honduras together. Back then, Nicaragua was our enemy. They were working with Russia to destabilize the region. Pat and I were omega team leaders. We each ran small patrols of four or five NCOs along the border between Nicaragua and Hondo.

"One night, Pat was set up at an ambush site with his guys and I was still moving into position with mine. It was dark. The part of the jungle we were working in was really thick. I was leading the patrol, walking down a trail, ready to put my guys into an ambush position, when suddenly I realized I was in the middle of an enemy kill zone. I was shot three times in the chest, and the rest of my patrol behind me was pinned down and couldn't move. Pat was with his guys more than a kilometer away. I was in the middle of the trail, bleeding badly, there were tracers and explosions everywhere.

"Pat told his guys to stay where they were, and in the middle of the night, he ran to me through the jungle. That's where those scars came from. He has them on his legs too. The black palm trees have three-inch spikes, and he ran through more than half a mile of them and then straight into an ambush. When he crossed the trail, starting from the end of the ambush line, he took out every single enemy fighter. I watched him. I couldn't move, but I saw it all. The tree cover went all the way across the trail. You couldn't land a medevac helicopter.

"When it was over, he picked me up and ran with me in his arms, like a baby, for more than three kilometers back to our base. The doctor told me if I had arrived five minutes later, I would have died from loss of blood. The big dumb galoot was bleeding like a stuck pig when he brought me in. The medics thought he got shot, but it was just the cuts from the black palm," Mike said.

"Did you return to the battalion after Honduras?" said Claire.

"Yeah," Pat said.

"Did you jump into Rio Hato?" Claire said.

"Yup."

"So, what's going to happen when Mike returns to D.C.?" Claire said.

"I have no idea. Mike is the brains when it comes to the swamp."

"But if something goes wrong, you'll get involved?" Claire said.

"With the exception of Hondo, it's always been Mike bailing me out of a tight spot. Mike's a boy scout. He believes in the system. What he's going to do is essentially be a whistleblower, which means he should be protected. Me, I'm not a boy scout. I have very little faith in the system. If Mike fails, then I'll take care of things my way," Pat said.

"What is your way?" Claire asked.

Pat smiled and signaled the waitress for another round of drinks.

Chapter 24

Washington, D.C.

Mike Guthrie went to meet with General Santos, the Director of National Intelligence, at his office in the Executive Building. His briefcase contained a copy of the Bellomo interrogation. He'd arranged the meeting through Steve Bonk, who was a former coworker in the Agency and a senior staffer to the DNI.

Mike was ushered into the DNI's office after only a short wait. The secretary walked him into the big office, which was empty, and into a smaller side office. When Mike entered, he saw the CIA director seated opposite him at a small round table. The secretary quickly ducked out of the office.

"Where's General Santos?" Mike asked.

"He's running late. I told him I needed you for a few minutes first. I'm afraid I have some bad news," Director Pasternak said.

"Sir, this briefing is specifically for the DNI," Mike said.

"Forget the DNI. Something more important has come up," said the director.

"What could possibly be more important?"

"Yesterday in Kandahar, JSOTF 616 was conducting an HVT mission to capture Akim Al Saraa. He's a Jordanian foreign fighter who has been leading much of the AQ resistance in the Province. DEVGRU had the main effort. Akim Al Shilabi was killed during the capture attempt. The Rangers were in support. They were cordoning the objective. We believe one of the Afghan National Police went hostile in a blue-on-blue situation. At one of the checkpoints, two of the Rangers were killed. A third went missing. I regret to inform you that missing Ranger is your son. Please understand, we're doing everything in our power to resolve this situation," said Pasternak.

Mike slid a chair out from behind the table and sat down slowly. He was speechless and deflated. The director poured him a glass of water and slid it across the table for him. Trying to gather his faculties, Mike gulped the water and returned the empty glass to the table.

"You son of a bitch," Mike said.

"Pat Walsh has gone rogue. He's killing innocents on American soil. We need you to help us take him down."

"I want to see proof of life."

"This tape was released by his captors this morning," Pasternak said. The conference room TV suddenly came to life. The video was taken with a cell phone. It showed Mike's son, still in uniform, bound by the hands and feet in a poorly lit room with a dirt floor. The young officer was dirty and dazed but did not appear seriously hurt.

"Look, there's no need for you to pretend. Tell me what it'll take to release my son," Mike said.

"This is clearly a difficult time. I suggest you bring your wife back to Virginia. We'll also need to know everything you have on the Pat Walsh's compound. As I said before, he's gone rogue and we're going to need to bring him in," Pasternak said.

"Okay."

"Call your wife and tell her to catch the next flight."

"Okay."

"Do it here, now," Pasternak said.

Mike withdrew his cell phone from his interior suit pocket. He hit the contact button.

"Honey, how are you? ... I briefed the DNI. Everything is okay.... I want you to hop on the next flight and return home.... Everything is fine.... Time to leave that black palm alone and get back home to your own garden," Mike said. The call lasted only a few minutes.

"She'll leave the Bahamas on the next flight this afternoon," Mike said.

"What can you tell me about Walsh's compound?"

"His house is made of stone. The compound has a guesthouse, a pool house and the main house. He spends most of his time in the office on the third floor of the main house."

"What about security?" Pasternak said.

"He hired a security firm. They have nine men who work eight-hour shifts, three at any one time. They're tasked with personal security for Diane. They don't guard Pat. They maintain a twenty-four-hour security perimeter around Diane," Mike said.

"What kind of weapons do they have?"

"They carry concealed pistols."

"You're officially suspended with pay, pending disciplinary action regarding your oversight of the illegal domestic activities of Pat Walsh. Go home, stay there, wait for your wife. Plans are currently underway to rescue your son and return him to you safely. The way I see it, your wife will return to Virginia, Walsh will be apprehended, and your son will be rescued—in that order," Pasternak said.

Mike left the DNI's office stunned. He stood in front of the elevator for a full five minutes before ever pressing the button for the ground floor.

Chapter 25

Eleuthera, Bahamas

Pat was sitting at his desk. Seated across from him was Jessica, the Trident office manager.

"The orders this month are a little lower than what we had the same time last year," Jessica said.

"We're supporting a conflict that's winding down. What did you expect?" Pat said.

Jessica was Korean American. She was five-two with short brown hair, brown eyes and a petite figure that was adorned with business clothing that could only be described as severe. Jessica was a workaholic with an incredible memory and a penchant for focusing on the tiniest of details. Jessica managed all of Trident's business operations.

Claire walked into the meeting. "I'm sorry to interrupt, but I need to talk to you."

"It's okay, you can talk in front of Jessica."

"Mike called me. He wants me to go back to Virginia. He's going to get me a ticket for this afternoon's flight. But something's wrong," Claire said.

"Why do you say that?" said Pat.

"It was a strange conversation. He said everything as okay. He mentioned gardening, and he mentioned black palm.

There's no black palm in Bahamas. It was a message of some kind. I just don't know what he meant by it."

"Do as he asks. I'm sure everything else will take care of itself," Pat said.

"You think so?"

"Definitely. What time do you want to be taken to the airport?"

"Three," Claire said.

"You better pack, I'll have someone drive you," said Pat, and Claire turned and left the room.

"Let's finish this later," Pat said.

"What's up?" Jessica asked.

"Trouble. Can Diane stay with you?"

"Yes, of course."

Pat walked the grounds of the house as the sun was beginning to set. After completing the walk, he entered the house through the back door and walked into the kitchen. Bob McCalister was seated at the kitchen table.

"What's the status?" said Pat.

"Diane is at Jessica's with one of my guys for security. Father Tellez, Jonah, and Maria are in Nassau. It's you, me and eight of my finest," said Bob.

"What's your best guess on how they'll come in?" said Pat.

"The water has calmed a lot. My guess will be rigid inflatables onto the beach," Bob said.

"The compound is fenced by some pretty tough vegetation. Do you think they might try to crash the front gate?"

"I think a beach landing is most likely."

"Are your guys up for this?"

"Our fee just tripled. My guys were all CT when they were with 22," said Bob in a barely intelligible Scottish accent, referring to the elite company of assaulters within the famed British SAS Regiment. "They won't disappoint."

The men spent the next two nights on alert, constantly fortifying the compound. On the third night, Pat's IMBITR radio chirped.

"Hotel Four, six bandits on the radar eight kilometers due east. They're being launched from a small ship," said the team manning the combined day, thermal and GSR surveillance system on the roof of the main house.

"Roger," said Pat.

"Hotel One and Two, report when you have visual," said Bob.

"Roger," said Pat.

"This is Hotel Four, we have three vehicles approaching from the west. Distance two kilometers."

"Hotel Three, did you monitor?" said Pat.

"Roger," said the two commandos dug into a two-man fighting position in the center of the front lawn.

"Bandits two klicks east on the water. Looks like two RIBs with crew served," said Hotel One.

"Roger, identified," said Hotel Two.

"Weapons free," Pat said. Hotel One and Two were both dug into two-man fighting positions in the pink sands of the beach. In each fighting position was an M2A1 50-caliber heavy machine gun. Looking through the BAE Universal Thermal Clip On sights mounted on top of the weapons, the gunners could easily identify the hot thermal signatures of the people and the RIB engines against the cooler water.

Unseen by the surveillance team on the roof or by the men in defensive positions were the two sappers who were placing demo breach charges on the compound's iron front gate. As the 50-caliber machine guns opened up on the beach, the gates to the compound blew wide open. The two men from the Hotel Three fighting position on the front lawn fired two AT-4 84mm antitank rockets simultaneously at the first armored Suburban as it was passing through the gate. The two 84mm high explosive rounds hit the front of the truck seconds apart, instantly turning it into a flaming wreck.

Only two of the six rigid inflatable boats managed to reach the beach. The constant movement on the water made it nearly impossible for the RIB machine gunners to hit anything, while the fires from Hotel One and Two with the more stabilized systems and better optics were deadly.

After being picked apart by the heavy machine guns, only six of the amphibious assaulters were able to bypass the two fighting positions on the beach and reach the main house. In the front of the house, the second Suburban met with the same fate as the first. Five personnel from the third and last vehicle were able to dismount. The five began a slow crawl toward the main house under heavy fire from the two commandos on the front lawn.

With the exception of the two-man observation post on top of the house, the only two people inside the house were Bob and Pat. The two men moved in synch, with Pat, the taller man, in the high position and the shorter muscular figure of Bob crouched in the low position. Hotel Four, the OP, called each penetration into the house, and Bob and Pat responded. Both men were carrying blackout 300 Troy rifles with PEQ 18 lasers. They were each wearing TYR PICO plate carriers with OPSCORE Fast Helmets hosting L3 PVS-18s night vision goggles. The Peltor headsets, fingertip push-to-talk switches and throat microphones allowed the two men to stay in constant communication as they covered each other while leapfrogging from room to room.

Every door into the house had a number and the OPs called out each penetration. "Two tangos, door five," said Hotel

Four. Bob duck-walked slowly, his weapon at the ready, with Pat walking behind him, his weapon over Bob's head. Bob's IR laser was moving from nine to twelve o'clock while Pat's danced from twelve to three. The two infiltrators entered the corridor and were instantly dispatched by a salvo of suppressed gunfire from both men.

"Hotel Four, door one, one tango." And the two men reversed direction and headed to the main foyer.

When the sun rose the next morning, all ten men were exhausted. The smell of cordite and burnt rubber from the boats and trucks hung in the air. The ground was littered with bodies, spent shell casings, ammo cans, and expended AT-4 tubes. The damage to the house was mostly superficial. Two of the big picture windows in the back were blown out, and bullet holes marked many of the exterior walls.

"What are we going to do with these bodies?" said Bob.

"How many are there?" said Pat.

"Eight men in each boat, so that's forty-eight, and another five per vehicle, so another fifteen, plus the two dismounts," said Bob.

"Sixty-five bodies," said Pat.

"We can only find twenty-nine. Two of those boats were sunk pretty far out. Two got shredded closer to shore, and two made it onto the beach. Two of the trucks are a mess, and there may be bodies that got cremated inside. Some of them must have escaped. We're going to need a professional cleanup team," said Bob.

"Put the bodies in the working boats and send them out to sea. I'm sure they have RFID or GPS, and the launch boat will recover them. I'll have a cleanup team here by the afternoon for the trucks and to fix the damage," Pat said.

"What about the police?" said Bob.

"It's a tiny force. They focus on protecting tourists. We have an arrangement—they won't come around. Plus, it's off season and nobody lives within half a mile. With the surf and wind, I doubt anyone even called the police. Although it might be a good idea to put the crew-served weapons and long guns back into the vault," said Pat.

"Who were those guys?" said Bob.

"Contractors. Must be one of the bigger guns-for-hire companies. Pretty well equipped, but not very skilled. I would say American, based on the equipment and how they look," Pat said.

"Do you know who hired them?"

"I have a pretty good idea."

"What's next?" Bob asked.

"You and your guys stay here. I don't expect any more trouble. I'm going to have a talk with the man who I believe is responsible," Pat said.

Chapter 26

New York City

Michael roamed his apartment. On the advice of Bill Pasternak, the CIA director, he had been barricaded inside his penthouse apartment for more than a week. The twelve-thousand-square-foot apartment was making him claustrophobic and irritable. He hated running on the treadmill. It was a poor substitute for his daily Central Park jog; he needed the competition. Adding to his frustration was his latest mail order. Justina, a dark-haired beauty from Lithuania, was proving herself to be a spoiled temperamental creature who so far had shown an uncanny ability to rebuff his suggestions to experiment sexually. By now, his girls were usually comfortable enough with him to be coaxed into visiting his purpose-built S&M chamber. The way he saw it, once they consented to enter the room, everything that happened after was his decision only. They were going to fulfill his needs whether they consented or not.

Strategic Security Solutions, or Triple S, was a military contracting company headquartered in Georgia. G3 had purchased the company eight years ago and had grown it into a major contractor to the Defense and State Departments. Triple S had a huge training compound near Athens, Georgia, that was used to train US and foreign government agencies in driving, tactics, CBRN defense, and weapons. Michael looked toward the door, where two men were standing guard. Both were members of his Triple S personnel security detail. The larger force was downstairs, in the lobby and on the street.

Michael was on the balcony, standing by the rail overlooking Central Park. The leaves on the trees were beginning to thin. In the early-morning light, he looked down at the autumn foliage blanketing the park. From this elevation, it was like looking at a huge carpet bursting with orange, red, yellow and brown. It was an arrestingly beautiful scene, and yet none of it registered with Michael. The cheap Nokia burner phone in his pocket rang, and for the first time that morning, Michael breathed a sigh of relief.

"What do you have for me?" he asked.

"The news isn't good," said Stanley Bilas, the CEO of Triple S.

"Tell me you didn't fail."

"It was a major battle. They knew we were coming. We estimate he had a force of between twenty and thirty men. They were heavily armed with machine guns and antitank rockets. It was a slaughter. I had thirty-two men killed and another sixteen wounded. Your intel was bad," Stanley said.

"What about Walsh? Was he there? Any chance he was taken down?"

"We're still debriefing the survivors, but it seems unlikely. Only a few of my guys ever made it into the house, and none of them came back out."

"The intel was solid. At most your men, went up against a force of eleven. How the hell did you screw this up?" Michael said before he terminated the phone call.

Michael could barely control his rage. He dropped the phone and crushed it with the heel of his Italian loafer. He walked into his office and booted up the laptop he reserved for communication with the CIA director. He hated the inconvenience of chatting on gaming sites. The World of Warcraft gaming community was probably the biggest collection of geeks and lunch money donors in the world. As far as Michael was concerned, the only positive purpose they served was to host his communications with the director. Today, he didn't expect to have to wait half a day for a reply to his message. He was sure Bill Pasternak was waiting for the news.

"!!!!" he typed.

"Is it done?" Pasternak replied within seconds.

"It was a total mission failure. The force was destroyed."

"What happened?"

"They were ready for us. Most of the force was killed before they ever got to the objective," Michael typed.

"That's a tactical error. The intel was good."

"You said it was nine guys with pistols. My men were mowed down by machine guns and rockets."

"We have to stop underestimating this guy," Pasternak typed.

"What's next?"

"He has a lot of evidence he obtained from your people in New York. His two options are to release that information either to the government or to the press. Destroy every link you have to the organization."

"What do you mean by every link?" Michael typed.

"I mean everything. We can survive an investigation. I've seen the tapes. The only people mentioned were you and the guys on the Armed Services and Intel committees. None of you'll talk, because if you do, you'll be lucky to get a life sentence. Nobody is going to make a deal with people at that level. Plus, the only person the politicians know is you. The only people I'm worried about are your fishing club. Those guys would be offered a deal, and they might take it. They need to go," Pasternak typed.

"Why am I suddenly feeling like the fall guy?"

"You're covered. Walsh is blocked. He doesn't have access to the president, and those tapes are too self-incriminating to turn over to the press. His only option is to leak some of the info on the tapes and provide a pathway for a reporter to corroborate. They can't publish without verification, which you're going to make sure doesn't exist."

"What about your own house?" Michael typed.

"We had one guy working with Walsh. He has been neutralized."

"I'll take care of things on my end."

"Notify me when it's done and keep your guard up," Pasternak typed.

Michael's agitation was over, and now he began to feel a sense of relief. Over the past several weeks, he had been under siege. It had gotten so bad he was now barricaded in his apartment. The deaths of Barney, Anthony and Nicky made him feel more vulnerable than he had in years. Now he saw the endgame. He had a way out. Walsh had done him a favor. The big dummy had eliminated three of the key witnesses against him. He had taken out the guys who posed the greatest threat to Michael. By killing Barney, he had also made it possible for Michael to regain full control of G3 and get out from under the family.

He wondered if he could somehow get the mindless grunt to take out Vogel, Cohen, Garthwait, Truesdale and Patterson for him. For the first time in days, a surge of optimism spread through Michael. He would call a meeting and have all five CEOs picked up by the same private jet. A tragic air accident would follow, and he would move to acquire the companies. If he couldn't get them onto the same plane, he would get them in a boat and do the same thing. He didn't think he could acquire them all, but any one of them would make a valuable addition to the G3 portfolio.

With renewed energy and confidence, he began to plot. He would solve his business problems today, and then he would fix that bitch Justina tonight. No more coy suggestions for her to visit his special room. It was time to grab the bull by the horns.

Chapter 27

Eleuthera, Bahamas

Pat watched the C-130J touch down on the single runway at Governor's Harbour. The aircraft taxied toward the small terminal building and came to a halt one hundred meters from his position at the base of the terminal. Pat waited for the back ramp of the aircraft to drop before beginning his walk to the aircraft.

The engines were going through shutdown procedure as he approached. The roar of the engines and the smell of the burning JP-8 fuel were familiar. Walking down the ramp wearing a headset was the perpetually grinning Migos. Pat shook Migos's hand and walked up the ramp into the cargo area. He was greeted by Bill Sachse, the crew chief, once he got inside the cargo area. The engines finally shut down, and the two pilots, Mark Burnia and Chip Hawthorne, came out of the cockpit to meet Pat.

"How long did it take you guys to get here from Cyprus?" Pat said.

"Almost eleven hours, not much of a tailwind," Burnia said.

"I'm sure you guys are tired. I have a van to take you to your hotel rooms. We'll depart tonight on your call. I need you to work out a flight plan that puts me over Central Park with a TOT of 0300 tonight," Pat said.

"We've already worked it out and filed the flight plan. Takeoff is 2115," Burnia said.

"What about the equipment?" Pat said.

Migos went to the back area and retrieved two parachute bags. "This is the RA-1 Military Free Fall Ram Air parachute you requested," he explained as he pulled the parachute from the bag by the harness.

"This is the helmet, mask and SOLR oxygen system. We couldn't get the newest one on short notice, so this is the MBU-12P mask, which I'm sure you've used before," Migos said. "This is the JTRAC NAVAID you wanted. This baby'll land you on a dime. That's everything you asked for. We also have some NODS and weapons in case you forgot to ask."

"That all I need. I'm going to take the JTRAC back and work with it. You guys should get some sleep. I'll meet you at eight thirty tonight," said Pat.

"Boss, when you program the JTRAC, you need to maintain some flexibility," Burnia said.

"What do you mean?"

"We're flying direct to Albany, and the flight path takes us over Manhattan. But it's a very busy airspace. The ATC could have us at ten, fifteen or twenty thousand feet. They also might redirect us. I'll keep you up to date in flight, but once we get into that airspace with Kennedy, LaGuardia and Newark, there's no telling how they'll manage us."

"That's why I'm taking the JTRAX back. I'm going to simulate as many scenarios as possible today. I'm sure it'll work out," Pat said.

"We have two sets of everything in case you need some help," Migos said.

"I have it covered, Migos, thanks for asking."

Pat walked into the aircraft at 8:15 as promised. He promptly lay down on a row of mesh nylon bench chairs and fell asleep. Migos shook him awake at 2 a.m. He dressed for the cold. He was wearing a dark grey Beyond A9 uniform with a black wind shirt and insulated layer underneath. It could be as cold as negative twenty Fahrenheit depending on at what altitude he exited, and he dressed for it with insulated boots, gloves and a ski mask. He was wearing a soft level 2 covert armor vest, and his weapons were a suppressed SIG 226 and a Benchmade 3300 BK automatic opening double-action knife.

He also wore a headset that connected him to the flight crew.

"TOT is twenty minutes. Jump altitude is twenty-two thousand AGL," said Burnia. Pat had the coordinates and the altitude to the top of the building already plugged into the JTRAX. The plane was going to travel directly over Manhattan; deploying his parachute at five thousand feet would get him through the cold quickly and still give him enough time to manage the precision landing.

Pat put his helmet on and connected his oxygen mask. The aircraft began to depressurize and the interior white lights changed to red. Ten minutes out, the ramp was lowered and Pat had his first look into the clear, cold abyss. Pat turned on his NODs and flipped them down to check, then flipped them back up, leaving them on. He was wearing a full face mask, which gave him a clear picture of his navigation system. Using the system was pretty simple. Once he deployed his parachute using the altimeter, all he needed to do was to keep the arrow on the direction to target line and he couldn't miss.

Pat walked to the edge of the ramp and turned in toward the cargo hold so he could see Migos. He received the thirty-second warning signal from Migos and did a last-minute systems check. When Migos signaled to jump, Pat fell backward into the night. He stabilized his position and began to freefall facedown. Moving two hundred and fifty miles per hour in minus twenty temperatures made for a chilly ride. He fell for almost ninety seconds. It was easy to spot Central Park. He adjusted his position and oriented toward the southeast corner of the big green rectangle in the direction of his target.

The winds were nine miles per hour from the south, which meant he had to open as close to the target building as possible because the forward speed of his canopy and the speed of the wind would mostly cancel each other out, and he wouldn't be able to get much forward movement once he opened. At five thousand feet, he deployed his chute. He checked his canopy, which blended beautifully with the dark sky. Using his toggles, Pat kept his azimuth on the direction to target indicator on his JTAX.

Early on, his vision occasionally shifted to spot the target manually, but as the target grew closer, he kept his focus on the NAVAID. At twelve hundred feet AGL, he was almost directly over his objective. He stopped using the NAVAID and now relied entirely on his view of the building top. The parachute was moving at a forward speed of less than two miles per hour as he descended the final few hundred feet to the top of the Michael Genovese's penthouse apartment.

Looking down, he could see a pool, a patio and a large garden area on the top of the building. He adjusted his aim for the garden. A sudden gust of wind caused him to overshoot and almost dropped him into the pool. He pulled down hard on his right toggle to pivot and ran with the wind just enough to make it over to the patio. He flared his parachute and made a running landing. He was barely able to collapse his chute before he ran out of runway and came perilously close to falling off the roof.

Pat quickly detached his parachute harness and oxygen system. He flipped down the night vision mounted on his helmet and scanned the rooftop. The only light was a flashing red aircraft warning beacon on top of the building. He removed the pistol from his shoulder harness and screwed the suppressor in place. As he walked around the pool to the doorway, he found a lone figure curled up in one of the patio chairs. The girl stared at him. She was seated with her knees to her chest and her arms wrapped around her knees. The girl must have seen his landing, yet she did not move or say a word. The temperature was barely above freezing, and the girl was not wearing a coat. As he got closer, he noticed trickles of blood coming from her nose and ears. Through his night vision goggles, the blood showed a darker green against her face. Her lips were split, and one of her eyes was swollen shut.

He flipped his night vision up and went down on one knee in front of the girl.

"Are you okay?" he said in a quiet voice.

"Do I look okay?" the girl responded in a foreign accent.

"Did Genovese do this to you?" Pat said. The girl nodded. "I'm going downstairs to kill him. Any problem with that?"

"He deserves it. Make him die," she said.

"That's the plan. Does he have any guards?"

"Two security guards at the front door. They sit where the elevator and staircase doorway open. The only time they leave is to go to the bathroom or the kitchen. I know because they're blocking me from escaping the apartment."

"Is there anyone covering the roof access door?" Pat said.

"No."

"Where's Genovese?"

"He's in bed," said the girl.

"How do I find his room?"

"When you exit the door, go straight and follow the corridor to the living room. The two guards will be to your left in the foyer. Cross the living room and turn right at the next corridor before you get to the kitchen. His bedroom is at the end of the hallway. Last room on the right."

"What is your name?" Pat said.

"Justina."

"It's cold. You shouldn't stay outside too much longer. Give me ten minutes and then come down. It'll be safe by then," Pat said. She nodded.

Pat left his night vision goggles up as he entered through the roof door and descended the stairs toward the main floor of the apartment. When he reached the door, he paused to listen for the guards. After a fifteen-second wait, he turned the doorknob with his left hand and flipped the safety on his pistol off with his right thumb. He stepped into the dark corridor and slowly walked toward the light where the corridor opened into the living room.

The rubber soles on his boots were soundless as he slowly advanced down the corridor. He paused at the end and listened. Still no sound from the guards. They might have heard the door, but most likely would have dismissed it, thinking it was Justina. He took two steps back from the end and gradually executed a pie move from left to right, opening up more of his view of the foyer as he moved from one side of the corridor to the other.

The living room slowly came into view as his vantage point grew. The first guard was seated, facing to Pat's left, where the elevator and the second guard was posted. With both hands on his pistol, Pat fired two quick rounds at the guard's head and stepped fully into the living room. He expected the second guard to be covering the elevator. However, while the chair was still there, the guard was not.

Pat quickly swung to his right toward the kitchen. The second guard had already unholstered his weapon, and the two men exchanged shots. Pat's round struck the man in the chest, causing him to drop. The guard's shot went high, but the boom from the unsuppressed pistol echoed through the apartment. Pat raced to the downed guard and put two rounds into the face of the dazed man as he lay on his back. He assumed the guard was wearing ballistic protection, and he wasn't about to take any chances of him getting back into the fight.

He walked past the kitchen and, using the same pie technique, cleared the corridor before stepping into it. He slowly inched his way to the end of the hallway and stopped at the last door on the right. He could tell from the outside that the room was dark. He expected the master bedroom in a luxury apartment of this size to be a suite with multiple rooms. He was going to have to clear each room methodically, knowing that Michael Genovese was going to be awake and waiting for him.

Pat slowly opened the door and stepped inside. He brought his night vision goggles back down in front of his eyes and scanned the room, right to left, near to far. The bedroom had two doors and a corridor. He went to each door and opened it. Both closets were empty. He stepped into the small corridor and inched forward. At the end of the corridor, he found two closed doors, one to his front and another to his left. He imagined one would take him into a bathroom and the other a walk-in closet. He decided to start with the one on the left.

The door opened inward as he entered the huge closet. He made his first step forward when he heard the door behind him open and felt the sting from a baseball bat crashing down onto his left shoulder. Rotating to his left, he quickly brought his weapon up to a fire position. His right hand exploded with pain when the bat hit his right arm and sent the pistol flying. With his left shoulder and right arm partially paralyzed, Pat stepped forward and closed the distance with the bat-wielding slugger.

The next swing hit him in the ribs, but he was too close for it to have much force, and he was wearing ballistic protection. As his chest bumped up against the big man, he drove his right elbow into the other man's face. With his weakened left shoulder, he followed with a left hook that connected with

Michael's chin. With both hands still on the bat, the big man used the bat as a spear and drove the barrel into Pat's stomach.

Breathless, Pat grabbed the shirtless man around the waist and crashed his helmet-covered head hard into the man's nose. He felt the man's knees buckle, and as he was sliding downward, Pat rapidly brought his right knee straight up with all of his might. Michael Genovese's jaw shattered in a sickening crunch. Pat let the man fall to the ground. He shut off his night vision and flipped it back up. He found a light switch and turned it on and surveyed the scene. With the feeling still returning to his hand, he picked up his pistol, removed the suppressor and returned it to his holster.

As he was dragging Michael into the living room, he noticed Justina in the hallway.

"You should clean yourself up and get out of here," Pat said.

"I don't have any money and I don't have anywhere to go."

"Where is home?"

"Lithuania."

"Do you know where he keeps his money?"

"He has a safe in his office," Justina said.

"Go clean up and pack. Find his wallet and use one of his credit cards to book your flight. I'll get you some travel money in a few minutes."

Pat removed his helmet and jacket. He tied up Michael Genovese and did a quick tour of the apartment. The space was huge, with more than twenty rooms. When he returned, Genovese was conscious. His face was bloody, his nose was bent at an angle and his jaw hung loose. The blood was running down his naked torso and onto his pajama bottoms. Even bloody and beaten, the man was a physical specimen, he guessed about two hundred pounds of knotted muscle. Even obscured by the blood, he could see that he had the kind of abdominals usually reserved for the covers of romance novels.

"Your lady friend needs some cash to get back to Lithuania. Where can I find it?" said Pat. Michael Genovese lay on his side, on the floor with his hands and ankles bound. He said nothing. Pat slowly screwed the suppressor onto his pistol.

"Last chance before I start blowing off body parts," Pat said. With the broken jaw, Michael was hard to understand, but eventually, he was able to guide Pat to a stash of cash he kept in one of his bureau drawers.

"Pull a scarf over your face and go directly to the airport," Pat told Justina.

"What are you going to do with him?"

"He has a lot of sins to atone for. I'm going to help him find redemption."

"Did you want to know what he did to me in that room?"

"Not especially," Pat said.

"He deserves the same."

"Just get out of here and let me worry about him. The next time a psycho sex predator tries to fly you across the globe, it might be a good idea to decline the ticket. How did you meet this pervert anyway?"

"On a website called Travel Companions," Justina said.

"Probably a good idea to cancel your subscription."

"No kidding."

The sun was rising when Justina finally left the apartment. On her way out the door, she told Pat the next shift of guards would be showing up at eight.

Pat found the keys to Michael's Mercedes S65L when he was looking through his desk. He took both laptops on the desk and threw them in a backpack.

Pat rode down the private elevator with Michael. The greatest risk for exposure was going to be the move from the elevator to the car. Pat was relieved to discover Michael had a reserved parking space right next to the elevator exit. He forced Michael into the trunk of the car and drove it out of the parking garage.

Four and a half hours later, Pat pulled into a Hampton Inn in Langley, Virginia. The hotel was roughly two miles from the front gate of the CIA headquarters. He left Michael in the car and walked a half a block down the street to an Enterprise car rental office. Minutes later, he pulled up next to Michael's Mercedes and cross-loaded him into the back of the Hyundai Santa Fe he had just rented.

"What did you do in there?" Pat said when he opened the trunk. The combination of vomit and urine was overwhelming to the senses. "I thought you were a Harvard boy. This is disgusting," he said sarcastically as he grabbed the still shirtless and shoeless Michael from behind by the ropes binding his ankles. Pat gave a mock salute to the closed-circuit camera covering the parking lot. He made sure Michael's cell phone remained on the front passenger seat, where he had placed it earlier.

Pat switched cars two more times on the drive south through D.C. He rented the last vehicle with a different alias and drove west on highway 66.

At a rest stop, he rented a cabin online in Luray, Virginia. It was a two-bedroom, two-bath log cabin that advertised itself on the internet as being secluded and having mountain views. It was already dark by the time Pat pulled up to the cabin and used the code he had been given by the rental agency to open the front door. Pat dragged Michael from the SUV toward the house. He stopped at a garden hose next to the driveway. He used his knife to cut away Michael's urine-and-vomit-soaked pajama pants. He then hosed Michael down in the cool autumn air and then did the same to the back area of the SUV.

Pat dragged the nearly lifeless Michael into the cabin and laid him on the floor in the kitchen.

"I went into that creepy room of horrors in your apartment and took some things I thought might be useful," Pat said. He withdrew a heavy leather collar, a length of chain and two padlocks. Pat secured the collar around Michael's neck and locked the end of the chain to it. He locked the other end of the chain to a heavy wooden support beam that separated the kitchen from the living room.

"You're a bargaining chip. The only way you're walking away from this is if you help me trade you for what I want," said Pat. The pain in his jaw, the dehydration and the near suffocation in putrid conditions had wiped Michael out. He was lying on his chest with his cheek cold kitchen floor, whimpering. Pat retrieved the two laptops he had taken from Michael's office from the backpack.

"How do you contact Director Pasternak?" Pat said.

"Fuck you," Michael mumbled through his broken jaw.

"It's going to be awful hard to negotiate a trade with the other side if you don't help me establish communications. Don't make me ask you again."

"Fuck you. You aren't going to trade me, you're going to kill me."

"If I was going to kill you, I would have shot you in New York City instead of bringing your disgusting stinking butt down here. Last chance. How do I contact the director?"

Michael had rolled onto his back and managed to sit up with his back against the support beam. With some energy restored, he glared defiantly at Pat, who was sitting on one of the kitchen chairs less than ten feet from him.

Pat withdrew his pistol and slowly screwed on the suppressor in full view of Michael. He took careful aim.

"Wait, wait, I'll tell you," Michael said. Pat fired a single round into Michael's left ankle. The scream was deafening. It was a roar that was so loud and went on for so long, Pat didn't think it possible with the broken jaw. Minutes later, when the wails and the sobs began to slow, Pat tried again.

"I'm still waiting for an answer," said Pat.

"Use the HP ThinkPad. The laptop password is Crimson14," Michael said.

After a few minutes Pat was ready to move on. "What's next?"

"Open Internet Explorer and get on the World of Warcraft website. Go to the chatroom. Log on as Mordor77, the password is 87jeet!!vqy. Send a private message to Vadorware16," Michael said.

"What's the all okay sign?" said Pat.

"There is none."

"He already knows you aren't okay. I'm sure he's already looking for you. It's important that I provide him the code so he understands that you're talking freely and holding nothing back. It'll give him the kind of urgency that we both want him to have."

"Three exclamation marks, that's the all clear."

Pat used a spoon and a piece of clothesline to fashion a field expedient tourniquet below Michael's left knee. The wound wasn't bleeding very badly; the bullet had mostly struck bone. He poured part of a water bottle into Michael's eager mouth.

"When you cooperate, good things will happen. When you don't, bad things will happen. Do you understand?"

"Yes," Michael said, looking desperate.

"The jaw, the ankle and the nose are all painful injuries. That pain is your baseline. It can get much worse before you pass out. I'm going to set up the camera, and we're going to conduct an interview. If you answer the questions honestly and completely, then I'm going to make that pain go away with a shot of OxyContin. If you don't answer the questions correctly, then I'm going to shoot your other ankle, then your knees and so on. Are you willing to cooperate?" Pat said.

"Yes. Yes. Please."

Pat interrogated Michael for six hours with the occasional break for water. The idea of corporate leaders and government officials conspiring to win government contracts was hardly a new one. The twist was the creative addition of foreign governments and nonstate actors to create conflicts that in turn resulted in an increased number of government defense contracts. Michael was able to explain how Pasternak and Vogel were driven partially by altruistic reasons and how their real motivation wasn't just to make money, but to guide US foreign policy to one of greater strength and influence.

"What I'm hearing is that somehow a thirty-something-year-old kid and the over-the-hill gang from the New York mafia hijacked US foreign policy and took over the defense industry," Pat said.

"Yeah," said an exhausted and timid Michael.

"That's a spectacular story, but nobody is going to believe it. I was going to send this tape to the papers, but it's too farfetched. How did CIA Director Pasternak get involved?"

"Rossi brought us Pasternak. He was a Langley analyst going nowhere when Rossi discovered him. Pasternak has a wife that spends, and he's very ambitious. He isn't very bright, but he's cultivated an image as an eccentric intellectual and he's very good politically. The president likes him. Rossi and some of the other members of the committee gave him the career support he needed to rise. They practically sold him to POTUS. I gave him financial support; his wife works at a think tank that G3 controls. She makes a million a year as a senior fellow, writing articles that support our cause," Michael said.

"What is the name of the institute?"

"It's the Marshal Institute for International Studies."

"What about the DNI? How did he get involved?"

"He isn't involved," Michael said.

"Who made the decision to kill Fouad Zhattari?"

"Pasternak gave me the time and the place. Triple S did the hit with the people they have in Syria working for the US government."

"Do you work for Pasternak, or does Pasternak work for you?" Pat said.

"Neither. We work together. I help him in some ways and he helps me."

"What about the hit against me in Brussels? Who ordered that?"

"I did," said Michael.

"Who told you where I was going to be?"

"That came from Pasternak."

"How did Pasternak get that information?"

"I don't know. He gave it to me, and I passed it anonymously to Rizzo," Michael said.

"Did Pasternak know you were funding ISIS?" Pat said.

"We never funded ISIS."

"You worked with them. That guy who blew up the Grand Square was ISIS. Why did you set me up for the Brussels bombing?"

"It was revenge. That thing you did last year cost G3 a lot of business. We lost huge contracts in Kuwait and Saudi Arabia because you took out our partners. It was payback," Michael said.

"You killed all those innocent people in Brussels out of vengeance toward me?" Pat said.

"No, the job in Brussels was also business-related. Setting you up for it was the vengeance part."

"Why did Pasternak help me after the bombing?"

"He didn't know I had set you up. He was angry about it. If he didn't support you, it would have looked suspicious. He was covering his own tracks to make sure nothing led to him. That's also why he had Fouad Zhattari killed."

A proper interrogation of Michael Genovese would take weeks. The scope of his activities was simply too vast to obtain in a single interview. Pat knew Pasternak would be searching for him; he was planning on it. It was why he had taunted him with where he'd left Michael's Mercedes. Still, with the resources of the US intelligence community behind him, it wouldn't take long. He needed to move.

Michael Genovese was sitting up with his back to the support beam. He was still chained to the support by the neck. The lengthy interrogation video captured his body from the chest up and did not show his nakedness, or the tourniquet below his left knee. Pat was seated next to the table on which sat the digital video camera used to record the interrogation. Next to the camera was his pistol. He stood from his chair, picked up his pistol and calmly shot Michael Genovese two times in the head and once in the heart.

He returned the two laptops to the bag, threw in his pistol, jumped in the SUV and headed to Union Station in D.C.

Sixteen hours later, Pat was on the Silver Meteor pulling out of the Jusup Station, in Georgia. The laptop was on his knees, and he was sitting on the couch in his one-bedroom train car. The file was too big to email, so he set up a Dropbox account and transferred it in. Mike Guthrie had been out of contact ever since returning to D.C. He had signaled something was wrong when he'd called his wife in the Bahamas. Pat assumed it was a warning about the attack, but it could have been something else. He hadn't slept since the flight on the C-130 to New York. He was exhausted when he hit the send button for the email to Mike with the Dropbox instructions. He stepped over to the bed with plans to sleep until the train reached Miami.

Chapter 28

Langley, Virginia

Bill Pasternak was in an unusually foul mood for a Friday morning in the office. He kept his eyes on the file in front of him and did not acknowledge Guthrie as he was ushered into the office by his secretary. Guthrie sauntered up to the desk undeterred and helped himself to one of the two chairs that sat along the front. After two minutes of ignoring Mike, the director shifted his gaze upward. Mike looked as if he had aged ten years in the last week. The stress of not knowing about his son was taking a heavy toll. The observation pleased Pasternak, and he smiled in a rare display of emotion.

"Why are you here? You're on suspension, in case you forgot," Pasternak said.

"You wanted me to tell you if Walsh contacted me," Mike said.

"Did he?"

"This morning I received an email from him."

"What did he have to say?" Pasternak said.

"He said if my son isn't released today, you're finished."

"Is that right? Finished, he said?"

"Yes. He also sent me a file. Would you like to see it?" Mike offered a USB drive to his boss. "He said that isn't the full video, just a sample."

For the next forty-five minutes, the two men sat in silence. Pasternak was uncharacteristically fidgety as he watched the interrogation of Michael Genovese. Mike was unable to see the screen, but he had previously viewed the video and he listened for the second time as Genovese recounted Pasternak's involvement in the death of Fouad Zhattari and the ambush in Belgium, plus a laundry list of other major crimes. While listening to the anguished confession of Mike Genovese, Guthrie studied the files on top of the director's desk. He saw Pat Walsh's military 201 file, his most recent psychological evaluation, his medical file, a stack of CIA files and reports many inches deep. All told, he guessed at least two thousand pages of Pat Walsh were organized neatly on the director's desk.

The director finished the video and turned his attention back to Mike. "You have breached our agreement. You were told not to contact Walsh. At this stage, I don't know what I can do to save your son."

"I didn't breach the agreement. I haven't had any contact with Walsh until this morning, and it was him that contacted me, not the other way around," Mike said.

"Then how did he know about the assault on his beach house ahead of time?"

"He must have figured it out when you had me bring my wife back all of a sudden. You have all his files. Look up his IQ. He's a lot smarter than he lets on."

"He's a smart guy, I'll give him that. He's also a raving psychopath," Pasternak said, tapping the file folder with Walsh's psych eval.

"I'm pretty sure the file says 'mild sociopathic indications,'" Mike said.

"Would you call what he did on this tape a mild sociopathic indication? Do you know what that crazy son of bitch did? He kidnapped Genovese and he drove him here, to

Langley. He parked Genovese's car less than a mile from where I live. He was sending us a message," Pasternak said.

"He was sending *you* a message. He knows where you live. There is no us."

"By us, I don't mean you. I mean the CIA."

"Pat has nothing against the CIA. He's coming after you. You're supposed to be the big brain, the super analyst. You have thousands of pages of his history in front of you, and you don't know the first thing about him. No wonder he's been beating you like a dirty rug," Mike said.

"He's a rabid dog and he needs to be put down. If you don't take care of him and destroy those videos, there'll be no hope left for your son. This isn't a negotiation. That is the offer on the table. Take it or leave it," Pasternak said.

"Let me help you understand Walsh, so you can put to use those brilliant analytical skills that vaulted you to the top of the CIA. Wait, what am I saying? Genovese explains in the video how you made your way to the top. Anyway, the first thing you should know about the guy who's living rent free in your head is that he values loyalty above all else. People who are disloyal, he calls Blue Falcons. If you had any experience in the military, you would know that a Blue Falcon is a buddy fucker.

"Now you were on Walsh's team, and you tried to have him killed, not just once, but twice. I was on the same team as you, and you rewarded my loyalty by killing the Rangers serving with my son and by capturing him and holding him hostage. Walsh is a bit crazy, and you have committed an unpardonable sin in his eyes. You have the files on the assassination missions he did last year against the Gulf Monarchs. You're going to be out of a job once that video hits the internet tomorrow morning.

"Once you're out of the Agency, you cannot afford the kind of security needed to protect yourself from Walsh. That's why he parked that car close to your home. He's coming after you. The only guy who can protect you from Walsh is me. And unless my son is returned to me by the end of the day, and unless your resignation is announced immediately, I fully intend to stand by and watch him give you the full NORK treatment," Mike said.

"The NORK treatment?"

"The North Koreans kill three generations for disloyalty against the state. Pat agrees with the idea. He thinks people are genetically predisposed to treachery and cowardice. He'll wipe your DNA from the face of this earth. Let's be honest here. Your life is already void. Best case for you is to resign, return my son, and go somewhere quiet and kill yourself. If you do that, you'll be remembered by your family and friends as a patriot instead of what we both know you really are," Mike said.

"Best case is the US government imprisons you for collaborating with a known terrorist. We conduct a search of the computer you received this email on, track down Walsh and kill him."

"You've been monitoring my communications and my movements since our last meeting. You know you won't find Walsh. It's Walsh who'll be finding you, and your children and your grandchildren."

"Think about your son," said Pasternak.

"Think about your own family. Once the video hits the internet, your tenure with the Agency will be over, as will your government protection. Walsh will get to you, of that I'm sure."

The two adversaries sat across from each other for a full five minutes without speaking. Mike was miserable. He hadn't slept well since his last meeting with Pasternak. His heart was racing, and it was only the terror of what would happen to his son that kept him from going over the desk and killing the director. Although he hadn't spoken to Pat about his son's kidnapping, he was sure Pat sensed something was going on or he wouldn't have emailed him the Genovese interrogation. Mike was sure the assessment of Pat he had given to the director was correct, at least up to the part about the NORK treatment—that was pure nonsense.

He could see the internal struggle going on inside the director. Mike had no doubt Pat would kill Pasternak in a very bad way if any more harm came to his son. Looking at the anguish on the man's face, it was clear that he was finally coming around to that very same realization.

"Get out of my office. You'll get confirmation of your son's release shortly," the director said.

Chapter 29

Miami, Florida

Pat woke in his small bed within the cramped confines of his cabin on the Silver Meteor. The clicking sound the train made as it rolled over the track was hypnotically relaxing. He was rested and hungry. He checked his watch and decided to wait. If the train was on time, he would be in Miami in half an hour.

He was still wearing the same uniform he had on for the parachute jump into New York City. He noticed the pants were living up to their wrinkle-free advertising. With the black coat and black boots, he didn't look all that conspicuous. He flipped open the laptop and checked his email. He had an email from Mike that was only a few minutes old. It was a phone number. He powered up one of his burner phones and tapped in the number.

"My son was recovered in Jalalabad an hour ago. He's on his way to Bagram now," Mike said.

"I didn't know he was missing. What happened?" Pat said.

"Pasternak staged a blue-on-blue and had him taken. He was using him to hold me in check."

"How did you get him released?" said Pat.

"I took that video you sent me, walked into his office and told him that if he didn't return my boy and resign from his position, it was going to play on YouTube."

"I had a sneaking suspicion that clip was going to be of some use to you. I wish you'd told me about your kid. I could've helped sooner."

"I don't think there was any other way I would have been able to get him released. That clip was perfect. What made you think to send it?" Mike said.

"I expected you to show the video to someone higher up and for Pasternak and the rest of his minions to be arrested. I didn't expect it was going to be needed as a bargaining chip."

"I was in a bad place—it was a lifesaver. I don't think I'll ever be able to repay you."

"With Genovese and Pasternak off the board, that still leaves us a senator, a handful of congressmen, some corporate CEOs, and don't think I've forgotten the lovely Natalia. They were all neck deep in this crazy scheme, and every one of them needs to pay," Pat said.

"Did Genovese give all of that up?"

"I have another six hours of video that you haven't seen. This thing is a long way from over."

"Our part is over, Pat. With Pasternak gone, I'll be back on the job soon, and we can finish this through official channels. The president isn't going to want any of this to be made public. The number I gave you is my personal cell phone number. I was placed on suspension and under official investigation by the Agency. I'm sure our conversation is being recorded, which means the personnel assigned to investigate me will have all the information needed to clear me and to tie up the remaining loose ends of this thing," Mike said.

"The Agency that tried to have me killed in Brussels, launched a full-scale invasion on my home in the Bahamas, and kidnapped my best buddy's son is now my friend—is that what you're telling me?"

"Those actions weren't the Agency. It was only Pasternak and a few others."

"Genovese handled the corporate and political players. I feel pretty confident he gave up all of those people under interrogation. Pasternak ran a different part of the operation. You can't let him walk. Genovese didn't know Pasternak's people and vice versa. Pasternak needs to be questioned," Pat said.

"In the past few weeks, you broke a lot of laws within the US border. Given the scope of this conspiracy and your part in finding it and cleaning it up, I'm sure the Agency and the US government are going to commend you for your actions. But if you snatch a CIA director, even a former CIA director, and sweat him, you're going to bring a world of hurt down on yourself. Pasternak knows a lot of secrets unrelated to this conspiracy. His interrogation will occur, I'm sure of that, but it has to be done officially, and not by you and your methods," Mike said.

"I'm not proud of my methods. I only use them when they're the only thing that will work."

"Hey, you got my boy back, and you didn't even know he was missing. I love your methods. I want you to come out of this mess intact, with your business and everything else unharmed. It's time to turn this over to official channels, so you don't wind up permanently as a fugitive."

"You don't think there's any chance the government will try to cover up this scandal by taking me out?" Pat said.

"You have six and a half hours of video that could blow up the republic, and you have proven yourself to be remarkably difficult to kill. Give the people in this town some credit. The smart play is to keep you on our side."

"What's next?"

"You and I should meet. I need a copy of the full video," Mike said.

"I'll put the video in your Dropbox account. Did you get confirmation that Pasternak resigned? I'm getting tired of looking over my shoulder."

"It might take a few days to get everything sorted out. Although it hasn't been announced, I'm certain Pasternak resigned. Whatever assets he had chasing you should have already been called off."

"Well, then, I'm going to grab Diane and finish my boating trip," Pat said.

"I'm hoping to be reinstated any day, and my first task will almost certainly be to write a report on this fiasco. I cannot do that without sitting down with you and conducting a debrief."

"I'm going to lay low until you're one hundred percent certain Pasternak's people are no longer chasing me."

"I'll be in touch with an update in a few days, and we can plan a meet," Mike said.

Chapter 30

Phuket, Thailand

Pat waited in the crowded airport arrivals area. Standing a full head taller than everyone around him, he spotted Mike as he exited the customs area. Mike was wheeling his suitcase, wearing shorts and a short-sleeved floral button-down shirt. The two men greeted each other, and then Pat led Mike out to the hired limo.

The car dropped them off at the small Marina on Na Yang Beach, which was only a five-minute drive from the airport. Mike carried his suitcase downstairs to unpack in the guest stateroom while Pat untied the yacht and got underway. Later, Mike joined Pat on the flybridge.

"Do you need me to do anything?" said Mike.

"The autopilot does pretty much everything. The Strait of Malacca is kind of crowded, so the radar warning will go off a lot. I set the warning range to five miles. Otherwise the damn thing would never shut up. The only reason to be on the deck is to make minor course corrections to avoid collisions," said Pat as he showed Mike the various controls.

"How far is it to Bali?"

"It'll take us three days. We're going to have to anchor at night."

"Why don't I get a couple of beers and we can begin the debrief?" said Mike.

"Works for me," Pat said.

Mike knew his way around the *Sam Houston*, having spent many hours aboard during the past several years. The weather was in the eighties, and since it was the dry season, the sky was only partly cloudy. The greenish-blue waters of the Andaman Sea were filled with leisure craft, ferries and sampan fishing fleets. They were passing one of the many small islands that dotted the waters. The islands were tiny, with steep rocky cliffs and lush vegetation that seemed to spring from solid rock.

Pat sat at the helm station on the flybridge, and Mike set a bottle of Tiger Beer down in front of him on the console and moved across from him to the bench chair on the flybridge table. Mike had a laptop computer on the table he was booting up.

"How do you want to do this, Pat?"

"How about we start at the ending? You never told me what happened to Pasternak."

"He resigned, and a month later he died in a car accident. He lost control of his car and ran into a concrete overpass. It was a rainy night, and he was going too fast. I'm sure he did it deliberately. He even died like a coward."

"What about the rest of the guilty political scrubs on the Armed Services and Intelligence Committees?" Pat said.

"None of them will run for reelection, but it's going to take a couple of years to purge them all."

"Why so long?"

"The president wants to keep the conspiracy a secret. Plus, I think he likes the idea of having members of congress and the senate in his pocket."

"What about the lovely Natalia?" Pat said.

"She's still on the job. There's no proof that she set you up," Mike said.

"I think she did. No one else could have. You better watch your back where that one is concerned."

"In something as big as this, there are bound to be people who helped unwittingly, and some small fry who'll get away. The reason we have debriefs and reviews is to be as thorough as possible, to make sure we keep those who get away to a minimum."

"Here's to another win for the home team," Pat said, and the two men clinked bottles.

"Where's Diane? I thought she was going to finish this trip with you."

"She and I are finished. Right now she's in Costa Rica. She finally joined the professional surf tour. Her corporate sponsor, as it turns out, is Trident," Pat said.

"What happened? I thought you two had something," Mike said.

"We did, up until she came too close to what I do for a living. Diane is a surfer girl. She believes in karmic retribution and all that kind of new age hippy stuff. After the attack in Bahamas, she had seen enough and went ahead and dumped me."

"Are you going to be okay?"

"I'm not really happy about it, but I can't really say as I blame her. I'll survive. I'm looking forward to getting out on the open sea and working through the crossing. You know, keeping the engines going, planning the route, navigation, cleaning, food, just the basic stuff. It's a great decompressor. It's totally cathartic. I appreciate you coming out, by the way. I know you're really just here to check up on me. We could have done this by email," Pat said.

"Spending a few days on the water, fishing, drinking beer, grilling food on company time, is a pretty good deal. We've earned it. I'm going to take a few hours this afternoon to finish the debrief with you, and then I'll write the report tomorrow morning. After that, you can show me what it is about this boating lifestyle you find so appealing."

"Once you try it, you'll be hooked. I have scuba gear, surfboards, fishing rods, guns, beer, scotch, wine, you name it. This is going to fun," Pat said.

"Doesn't it ever get boring?"

"With the satellite, I always have communications. Even when I'm out on the water, I keep up with Trident. On this trip, I'm planning to surf some of the legendary spots in Indonesia, Micronesia, Polynesia, Hawaii, California and Mexico. It's the opposite of boring."

"It's a lot of time to be alone," Mike said.

"Solitude is fine with me. At work, I trade guns and financials, and when it comes to recreation, it's all solo sports. I'm pretty much a loner when you look at it," Pat said.

"You have the hormone levels of a pubescent fourteen-year-old. I don't think you could survive being alone for too long."

"I like to think of myself as a raging heterosexual. It's a medical condition I have learned to live with," Pat said.

"What are you investing in these days? Still riding the bitcoin bubble?"

"I got out of bitcoin. Although I'm not sure if that was a bubble. I don't think anybody understands why the prices move one way or the other on bitcoin. My latest speculation scheme is with the euro. It's been steadily rising over the past few months compared to the dollar, and when you look at the direction the two economies are taking, it makes absolutely no sense. So, I'm shorting the euro big-time," Pat said. "What about you, Mike? Have you had enough of government work? Are you ready to join Trident?"

"I'm going to stay on the Middle East desk. I'm not ready to hang it up just yet. Although if you asked Claire that question, she would probably give you a much different answer," Mike said.

"How do you stand those swamp creatures? Did you see the latest leak from the State Department? Someone actually gave the *New York Times* the details on the shipments of weapons through the UAE to Syria," Pat said.

"There's a lot of dissention right now. One group within the State Department is supporting Saudi and UAE in their dispute with Qatar; the other group is supporting Doha. Both sides are dumping secret information to the press to embarrass the other side. That's why we need you and Trident more than ever. We were never able to fully trust the political class, but now the civil service, the lifelong bureaucrats, are in rebellion and behaving the same as the politicians. That's why I need you to step up. The future is going to require more off-the-books programs that the politicians have no oversight of and programs executed by people outside the view of the bureaucrats so they can't sabotage them with their stupid deep state protests and other petty squabbles," Mike said.

"I'll keep Trident going as long as you want me to. I owe you."

"I had some discussions with the DNI about Trident. He wants me to expand your role beyond logistics. In his words, you have shown imagination and operational capabilities that in some ways exceed what we can do in house. If you're up to it, I'll occasionally send you some work beyond simply delivering weapons and ammo."

"I'm open to that. I'll probably need to beef up my team. I'd need a few more guys like Migos. If you know anyone, send them my way," Pat said.

Pat dropped Mike in Denpasar International in Bali after three days as planned. Two months later, he landed in

California. The early-winter weather in the Pacific was rough and stormy. Pat was exhausted when he tied down at the Bay Club Marina in San Diego, but at the same time, he felt refreshed. He had a full beard, red eyes from too little sleep. The nagging pain from the bullet wound in his thigh, the bruising in his ribs and arms, were all fading memories. His plan was to provision the boat and continue through the Panama Canal, then return the boat back to its place in Bahamas. It was almost time to go back to work.

THE END

43463743R00127

Made in the USA
Lexington, KY
28 June 2019